Double Miracle at St. Nicolino's Hospital

Where pioneering surgeries lead to happily-ever-afters!

Leon Cassanetti, Lizzy Beckley,
Giovanni Lombardi and Autumn Fraser—
four of the world's top ante- and neonatal surgeons
brought together to St. Nicolino's to perform
lifesaving surgeries on conjoined twins. With four
strong opinions and four different approaches,
they must put aside any professional differences
and work together to bring the very best outcome
for these baby girls.

But outside of the operating room, passions run even
higher when the pressure of performing miracles
proves life changing for all involved…

Discover Leon and Lizzy's story in
A Family Made in Rome
by Annie O'Neil

Read Giovanni and Autumn's story in
Reawakened by the Italian Surgeon
by Scarlet Wilson

Both available now!

Dear Reader,

When I was asked to write a duet with my fellow medical author Annie O'Neil, I jumped at the chance. Brainstorming about a hospital set in the beautiful city of Rome with two hunky Italian doctors gave us plenty to talk about—not that we needed it! Writing a story with a friend is always such good fun, and when I got lost at one point, she sent me a paragraph that summarized things so succinctly I started typing straightaway!

I also found a very inspiring picture of a handsome Italian doc that I pinned to the top of my computer and sent to my editor, Carly, too! I hope you enjoy Autumn and Giovanni's battle to reach their happy-ever-after as much as I enjoyed writing it. Please feel free to contact me via my website, www.scarlet-wilson.com.

Happy reading!

Scarlet x

REAWAKENED BY THE ITALIAN SURGEON

—

SCARLET WILSON

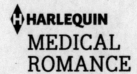

MEDICAL
ROMANCE

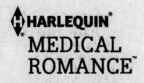

HARLEQUIN®
MEDICAL
ROMANCE™

Recycling programs
for this product may
not exist in your area.

ISBN-13: 978-1-335-40447-3

Reawakened by the Italian Surgeon

Copyright © 2021 by Scarlet Wilson

This edition published by arrangement with Harlequin Books S.A.

For questions and comments about the quality of this book,
please contact us at CustomerService@Harlequin.com.

Harlequin Enterprises ULC
22 Adelaide St. West, 40th Floor
Toronto, Ontario M5H 4E3, Canada
www.Harlequin.com

Printed in U.S.A.

Scarlet Wilson wrote her first story aged eight and has never stopped. She's worked in the health service for twenty years, having trained as a nurse and a health visitor. Scarlet now works in public health and lives on the West Coast of Scotland with her fiancé and their two sons. Writing medical romances and contemporary romances is a dream come true for her.

Books by Scarlet Wilson

Visit the Author Profile page
at Harlequin.com for more titles.

There's really only one person I could dedicate this
book to and that's my fellow author Annie O'Neil,
who made brainstorming about
hunky Italian doctors such fun!

CHAPTER ONE

IT HAPPENED IN the blink of an eye. Or maybe it was in a few seconds. But as Autumn watched her colleagues Sharon and Gavin turn to each other and laugh during the father of the bride speech she saw something.

It was like a giant neon sign pointing to the new bride and groom. The way that they looked at each other at that exact moment. The love. The connection. The promise. The life they hoped for together. All in that precise split-second.

Autumn Fraser swallowed, her mouth instantly dry as she smoothed her hands down the coral silk of her bridesmaid dress. She automatically reached for the glass in front of her and gulped quickly, almost wincing at the slightly warm white wine.

It had been a fairly relaxed wedding, meaning that by the time the speeches had rolled around, she'd moved from the top table to sit next to Louis, the man she'd lived with for the last year.

Life was comfortable. Her job as a specialist paediatric surgeon meant she was frequently jetting off around the globe to assist in difficult surgeries. Louis was equally busy as a specialist neurosurgeon. Sometimes they were like ships passing in the night. They'd met a few years ago and had fallen into an easy relationship. She liked him. She really did. But at this moment her heart was doing uncomfortable things inside her chest.

She glanced sideways and noticed that Louis, too, was watching the bride and groom closely.

'We don't look like that…' Her whisper was barely audible. She couldn't actually believe she was saying out loud the words that had been circling around in her head for months.

Louis's eyes didn't meet hers. 'No,' he said softly. 'We don't.'

It was an admission from them both. Part of her felt relief that he knew it too, but a little part of her felt empty.

Now her stomach was flipping over, joining the bedlam that was currently going on in her chest. It was the recognition. The agreement. Thank goodness she was sitting down, because she wasn't quite sure if her legs were up to the task of standing.

Silence hung between them. She blinked back tears. She wasn't sad. Truly, she wasn't. But

Louis was a nice guy. An intelligent companion who made her laugh, who was thoughtful in lots of ways, and every bit as annoying in others.

The last thing she wanted to do was hurt him. The thought of doing that really pained her. But was it actually more painful to meander along in a relationship that wasn't right for either party?

They'd drifted along over the last year—their relationship was a convenience. She'd moved in with him, but left her own place unrented. Now she was wondering why she'd done that. Had she always known, deep down, that it would come to this?

Her parents had had a tight, restrictive marriage. It had rubbed off on her. She couldn't pretend that it hadn't. Control was everything to her. And falling in love—*really* in love—That wasn't control. She was a surgeon. Losing her heart and her head just wasn't on the agenda for her.

Which was why she felt so confused right now. Because that look that Sharon and Gavin had just exchanged was pure, unadulterated love. And she wanted *that*. No matter how much she pretended she didn't.

Maybe it was the fact that she'd had a glass and a half of wine that was allowing her to peek through the shutters she normally had firmly closed around her heart, but the realisation was startling. And upsetting.

Her parents had never directly shown love to her, her brother, or to each other. In fact, they'd been rapidly admonished for any outward show of emotion. Joy, love, pain had all been buttoned up and kept inside. Both of them had been so focused on their academic careers. There had been no room for emotion. They'd thought everyone should only strive to be the best, and put all other sensations aside. There was no room in life for emotions. It was energy best spent elsewhere.

That was what she'd always been taught. But something was making her do this. Something was making her hear the words that were circling in her head.

Autumn's heart ached a little as she turned to face Louis. It was almost as if the realisation had crumpled his face.

His voice was deep and cracked when he spoke. 'I want that, Autumn. I want what they have.' He was glancing back at Gavin and Sharon, who were holding hands and laughing again at another joke.

She let the surgeon side of her brain take over. The part that was decisive and direct. It was so much easier than the emotional side, which was threatening to tip her in a direction where she might end up a blubbering wreck.

She slid her hand over Louis's. 'I want that for you too,' she said simply, working hard not to let her voice waver. 'It's time. We both know it's time. I'll go back to my own place.'

She didn't wait for a response. She just picked up her phone and walked out of the reception venue. She refused to let the tears that were brimming in her eyes slide down her cheeks. She wouldn't admit it out loud, but right now it felt as if a huge weight had just slid from her shoulders.

Giovanni Lombardi took a deep breath as his daughter Sofia climbed up into his lap. It was a hot, sticky evening in Rome. It didn't help that the air-conditioning he'd paid a fortune for a few years ago had decided to make some strange whirring noise and then clunk to a halt. He'd flung the villa's shutters wide, but there was no breeze outside—just more warm air.

Sofia was the equivalent of a hot water bottle, but Giovanni clutched her closer. She was his lifeline. The most important person in his universe. He would happily allow his body temperature to reach stratospheric heights in order to continue this moment.

His wife had died four years ago in a scooter accident on the roads of Rome. For a few months it had seemed as though the world was crumbling around Giovanni. Sofia had been his only reason for continuing.

'I like this one, Papà,' she said, pointing at a picture on the screen.

Giovanni was tired. He had one of the biggest cases of his career at St Nicolino's, the prestigious children's hospital in Rome where he was Chief of Surgery. His hospital—because that was how he thought of it—was renowned across Italy as a specialist hub for paediatric surgery and antenatal care, and five short weeks ago he'd been referred a case of conjoined twins, picked up at twenty weeks.

Most cases were picked up earlier than that, so he'd focused all his attention on making sure this family had the best antenatal care possible. His colleague, maternal foetal medical specialist Leon Cassanetti, had recruited Lizzy Beckley to partner with him in their birth. Now it was time for Giovanni to find a partner to work alongside him on the separation surgery.

He knew this case would have worldwide coverage. He didn't doubt he could persuade any surgeon, from any country, to be part of this surgery. Some surgeons he knew would probably fight over a surgery like this one. But picking the *right* surgeon was the priority here.

Whoever he picked would have to be happy to halt their life and come to Rome for at least the next four months. They would have to work alongside Giovanni and around fifty other members of the team to plan for this surgery. They would have to be happy to spend hours on research, hours on techniques specific to this case, with numerous practice surgeries. They would also need the ability to win the trust of the parents.

Giovanni already knew he would lead one team, and whoever he picked would lead the other. He had to trust them—he had to have faith that they could work alongside him, think the way he did, almost be in complete unison with him if they wanted both of these babies to survive. It was vital to pick the right person.

He had the details of hundreds of surgeons worldwide, and had spent the last two weeks filtering through them to find someone with the skill set and temperament that he needed. Volatile wouldn't work. Distracted wouldn't work. Passion and commitment were the absolute minimum of his expectations.

He leaned forward and inspected the photo that Sofia was pointing to. 'Ah, yes,' he murmured to his daughter. 'Her name is Autumn. She comes from Scotland.'

He had eventually streamed his list down to ten potential surgeons. All brilliant. All capable of performing the surgery. But Autumn Fraser was actually neck-and-neck with another one at the top of his list.

'Scotland… They have castles,' said Sofia. She leaned into his neck. She was clearly getting tired. 'Do you think they have fairies in the castles in Scotland?'

He smiled and ran his fingers through her dark curls. 'I think they might have.'

'She's pretty,' Sofia replied.

Giovanni blinked. 'Is she? I hadn't noticed.'

He leaned forward to take a better look at the photo. The truth was he hadn't really looked closely at any of the photos of the candidates. He'd narrowed his potential field based purely on experience and skills. The faces hadn't even implanted in his head.

As he leaned forward he tilted his face naturally to the side. Autumn Fraser *was* pretty. Maybe even more than pretty. Her hair was similar to Sofia's. Dark and shiny with a hint of a curl. But he'd missed the searing green eyes completely, and her skin, with a hint of a tan and a few freckles scattered across her nose.

His gaze went back to those eyes. Sincere, compassionate, with a hint of fun. He blinked again and gave a shudder. He couldn't remember the last time he'd considered a woman so closely. It made him uncomfortable. He'd lived his life in a bubble these last few years, with no room for thoughts like this.

'What's wrong, Papà?' asked the sleepy voice on his shoulder.

'Nothing, honey.' He ran one hand down Sofia's back as he flicked back to the list of surgeries Autumn had performed. She was a specialist in abdominal and liver surgery on tiny babies. Her record was good. She'd published several papers on technique, and presented around the world on improving outcomes in these children.

People often assumed that the separation surgery was the most dangerous moment in separating conjoined twins. Those with more experience realised that, whilst separation was difficult, patching up two separate babies, often with completely different medical issues, and giving them a chance of the best possible life was much, much harder.

Giovanni sighed and flicked back to the details of the only other surgeon who could rival Autumn's stats. He'd only just started scanning them when something sparked in his brain. He flipped back to Autumn's page. Yes. There it was.

He'd skimmed the list of publications, assuming they were all surgery-focused. But, no. Here was another with Autumn's name on as lead researcher: *Psychological Trauma and its Effects on the Separation of Conjoined Twins. A Twenty-Year Study.*

He froze. He hadn't seen that before. A quick date-check showed it was listed on her bio, but due to be published in a renowned surgical journal in two months' time.

Giovanni smiled. Separation trauma had long since been in his thoughts for these children. So far he'd been involved in ten separation surgeries for conjoined twins, and this was entirely the area of research he'd wanted to pursue next.

It seemed that his potential colleague had beaten him to it.

He picked up Sofia and carried her to bed, tucking her in and placing a gentle kiss on her brow.

Once he was sure she was settled he moved back to his desk and picked up his phone.

It seemed he'd found his perfect fit.

Autumn's neighbour flung open his door and screwed up his face. It seemed to take him a few moments to place her. 'Autumn…?' He looked her up and down, his expression clearly saying that he thought he was in some kind of weird dream.

She still had the flowers in her hair. The long, slightly stained coral bridesmaid dress in place. The light rucksack in her hand only carried some make-up, her phone, her purse and credit cards, and her laptop—which she never left the house without—along with a sewing kit for wedding emergencies and some chocolate. What it didn't carry was the key to her flat. That was back at Louis's house.

'What are you doing here?'

'Sorry for the late call. I need access to my flat and forgot my keys. Do you still have the spare set for me?'

Barry didn't move. It was as if her words hadn't quite sunk in yet. He screwed his eyes up again and shook his head slowly. 'What have you done? Run away from some kind of wedding?' Then his eyes widened and his mouth moved into a perfect 'O'. 'Did you run away from your *own* wedding?'

Autumn shook her head and extended her hand, palm up. She hadn't seen Barry in over a year. But it was late. And she was tired. And she was kind of hoping that there might be a bottle of wine still in her flat. There was a good chance that any tinned or packet food would be out of date. Teabags and coffee would likely be the only things of use.

Barry was still looking at her. 'Actually, can I be a pest?' she asked.

'What…?'

'I'd really appreciate a couple of slices of bread and a tin of baked beans if you have them.' She shot him her best smile.

Barry blinked in stunned silence, then she saw him give himself a visible shake.

'Keys,' he muttered as he walked back into his kitchen.

She heard the opening of drawers and cupboards before he returned with her keys clutched in one hand, and a plate with two slices of bread, a can of baked beans and a couple of digestive biscuits in the other.

Autumn sighed in relief. 'Thanks, Barry—much appreciated.'

'Do you need milk?'

She shook her head. 'No, thanks. I'm fine.' Her phone vibrated in her bag.

'Does this mean you're moving back in?' asked Barry as she started to back away.

It did. Didn't it?

Autumn kept the smile pasted on her face, even though her muscles were starting to ache. 'Yes, I will be. Nice to see you again, Barry.'

He gave a gentle nod and then, with a final glance at her dress, closed his door.

Autumn stuck her key in the lock and walked into her flat. As she breathed a big sigh of relief, she tried to ignore the slightly stale air. It appeared that the automatic air freshener she had plugged into one of the sockets had run out of scent.

The air was still warm outside, so she flung

the main window open wide and threw her bag
on the sofa. After some moves that could have
competed with a contortionist, she managed to
let the coral dress drop to the floor at her feet.

Many of her clothes were now at Louis's. She
still had some supplies here—generally the kind
of tired and boring clothes she hadn't worn for a
while—but there was a pair of comfortable pyjamas that she slid into after standing under the
shower for a few moments.

As she emerged back into the kitchen a
thought sprang into her head. She hadn't actually
said goodbye to Sharon and Gavin. *Oops.* But
Sharon would likely not be too worried about the
disappearance of one of her four bridesmaids.
She would probably think Autumn had been
called into work. It was fine. Autumn would
send an apology tomorrow and tell them to enjoy
their honeymoon.

Five minutes later she'd slumped on the sofa
with her beans on toast and cup of tea when her
bag made an odd noise. The phone. Of course.

She pulled it from her bag and frowned at the
unfamiliar number. She'd missed three calls.

It was late. Autumn was drained. She'd been
up since six this morning, helping Sharon get
ready for her big day. She took a few bites of
her food as she considered whether to call back.

It was as if someone was watching her. The

phone started buzzing again. Autumn wasn't on call, but she often had calls regarding issues with newborns when she wasn't on duty. Her body reacted on automatic pilot and she answered, switching her mobile to speaker.

'Autumn Fraser.'

There was a pause. Had the caller actually not expected an answer at this point? Then there was a voice.

'Hello? Ah, good, Dr Fraser, I think I'm about to make you the offer of a lifetime.'

The voice was heavily accented, warm as treacle, and instantly had her attention. 'Excuse me?'

There was a gentle laugh at the end of the phone. 'Forgive me. This is Giovanni Lombardi, Chief of Surgery at St Nicolino's in Rome. I'm sure you've heard of us.'

This voice was assured and confident. Part of her wanted to cut off this stranger and tell him she'd never heard of his hospital and to contact her secretary on Monday if he wanted to chat. Who had handed over her personal mobile number?

But of course she wouldn't. She was far too curious already. The caller had addressed her as 'Dr'. She was a surgeon, and professional courtesy meant she should be addressed as Ms or Miss. But she knew that those in her own profession in other countries were sometimes addressed as 'Dr'.

She took a deep breath. 'What exactly do you want, Mr Lombardi?'

The soft laugh continued. 'Well, if you'd read the emails I've sent you over the last few hours, you would know exactly what I want.'

She bristled. Who *was* this guy? That sounded like a telling-off. Whoever he was, he clearly didn't know her at all.

'Guess what…' she paused as she tried to remember his first name '… Giovanni? This might come as a surprise, but I haven't sat around all day, waiting for random emails to fill my inbox. I've been off duty at the wedding of a friend. I didn't expect to answer my phone or read any emails today.'

Autumn was aware that the more tired and exasperated she was, the more clipped and thick her Scottish accent became. She made no apologies for it, but in her head she could almost picture this man's puzzled face as he tried to interpret.

She was already feeling out of sorts. Dumping a perfectly nice and safe man and moving back home to her flat without thinking things through properly had put her on edge. She knew that when she woke tomorrow morning she'd have to grab as much control of the situation as she could. That was if there was any left.

Annoyed with herself, she pulled her laptop from her bag and flipped it open. It only took a few seconds to come to life and she could see a stream of emails. She opened the first and leaned forward.

What?

Her eyes scanned that one and her finger automatically pressed for the next. This one contained details of scans. The next, measurements.

He must know exactly what she was doing, because a few moments later his smooth voice asked, 'Do I have your attention now, Dr Fraser?'

He was toying with her. And, whilst he might sound like some kind of dreamboat, she *so* wasn't in the mood to be played with.

Her heart-rate was quickening. And her breathing. So much detail. So much information. Two precious little girls, connected at the heart and the liver.

'How was this missed?' she asked as she kept on reading, her mind pushing everything else away and focusing on the case in front of her.

'The babies had their arms around each other in the scan at eleven weeks. It was a newly qualified sonographer who thought they were just hugging.'

There was so much she could say right now, but what would be the point? Time had already been lost. 'You have them with you now?'

'I have them,' he said reassuringly. He paused, and then continued. 'After delivery I'm leading the separation surgery. I'd like you to lead a second team,' he said.

Her heart leapt in her chest. She didn't care that it wasn't anatomically possible, she would swear in any court that she'd just felt it.

A smile crept across her face. 'Of course you would,' she said, trying to sound as confident as he had earlier. She needed to be a match for this man in every way. Surgeon's rules: *always believe you're a match for any other one.* 'No one else has the experience of liver surgery on neonates that I do.'

She was on her feet, flicking the phone to speaker, striding through to her room and dropping it on the bed as she pulled her suitcase from the top of the wardrobe.

Giovanni Lombardi gave an amused laugh. It seemed to be his signature. She was trying to picture this Italian man with the tantalising voice in her head. The last thing she needed in a case like this was any distractions—particularly when preparation time was at a minimum.

'There were a few others….' he said, as if trying to keep her in her place.

'Rubbish. You wanted the best. You've asked me. And, luckily, I've just made myself available.'

She rattled off a whole list of demands. None of them were outrageous and she knew it. This kind of surgery was history-making. She was almost sure this hospital in Rome wouldn't deny her anything. And for some strange reason—as crazy as this was—it made her feel as if she was grabbing a bit of control back from her day.

He replied quietly with an assured 'si' to all her requests.

'I pick my own team,' she said as she threw random clothes into her bag. Her best work suits were at Louis's—as were most of her everyday items. She was left with half-full cans of deodorant, tubes of toothpaste and bottles of shampoo. Ordinarily she would have collected all her things herself, but it looked as if she might have to ask a delivery company instead.

'Of course you do. I have many staff you may feel are appropriate, but the assembly of any team is always down to the lead surgeon.'

'Great. What about flights?'

'I took the liberty of booking you a first-class flight tomorrow from Heathrow.'

She froze momentarily. He was presumptuous. But of course he was. No surgeon in their right mind would say no to this surgery. But she had her own tricks up her sleeve.

'Won't be necessary.' She grinned. 'I have my own transport available. I'll make arrangements right now. Expect me in Rome by early morning.'

Even though he couldn't see her, Autumn had a little fun by tossing her hair over her shoulder. Having a very famous billionaire brother was something she generally kept to herself. But she knew she could give Ryan a call and his company would file a flight plan and she'd be able to take off in a few hours. He was proud of her and her achievements, and he often helped her with travel arrangements when she needed to get to a place for work. He was one of the few people who understood her need to be in control.

Ryan had gone the opposite way. He'd left home, got away from their parents and lived a crazy life. No rules. No regulations. But then he'd made a discovery—one that had made him a billionaire. And instead of running from control he'd started to embrace it—in a good way. Along the way he'd met the perfect wife and had the perfect family. He'd even employed a few old friends he trusted to be part of his company. But all his money had kept his feet firmly on the ground, and he never forgot to check on his sister. He'd do anything for her.

'You will manage to get here by then?' asked Giovanni Lombardi.

'Absolutely,' she said with confidence. 'How about I meet you at the hospital at nine tomorrow morning?'

'Nine a.m.,' he agreed, although he certainly sounded a little bewildered.

She kind of liked the fact she'd thrown Mr Smooth off his game.

But it seemed he had a good recovery. 'You understand, of course, that before we formalise things I'll need to make sure that you're the right fit for the team.'

Heat rushed into her cheeks. That sounded completely personal. And it was. For a procedure like this, staff had to work in unison. It didn't matter that she and Giovanni would have teams of their own. They still had to fit together.

'I've never had a problem fitting in with a team, Giovanni.' She used supreme effort to try and mimic his smooth way of talking. 'Surely you can't be that difficult?'

The laugh she heard this time was deep and throaty. Every hair on her arms stood on end.

'Bravo,' he said. 'Or should it be *touché*?' There was a pause, and then he asked, 'Don't you need to clear this with your hospital?'

'No,' she answered quickly. 'I am literally a free agent. I have a sponsor. So, although I'm based in London, as long as I don't have surgical commitments and any current cases I am free to go to any case worldwide if it interests me and needs my skills.'

'That's a pretty unique arrangement,' he said quizzically.

'It is,' she agreed. 'But my sponsor gets credit in any research I publish, and in any publicity around the cases.'

She could almost see him nodding, contemplating her words. 'Understood,' he said after a few moments.

Autumn took a deep breath. The truth was, the timing of this couldn't be better. She'd be away for four, maybe five months. It would give her a chance to move on. Louis too. She hoped he'd find someone who'd look at him the way he wished for. Someone to give him the connection that they'd never shared. The kind of connection that she'd just witnessed between her friends, which had made her feel lonelier than ever.

Was there a chance that she could find that too? She gave a little shiver and pushed the thought from her head. She had long ago decided that lifestyle would never suit her. Too risky. Too much open to chance.

She was about to get the opportunity of a lifetime with this surgery. All her focus needed to be on *that*. She'd arrange for a delivery company to pick up her things from Louis and bring them back to her flat. With her in another country, the process would hopefully be painless for them both.

'Is there anything else you want to ask me? There's still much to discuss about the case,' said Giovanni.

Autumn shook her head, forgetting he couldn't see her. 'No, I'd prefer to do that in person tomorrow.'

'Then I'll be delighted to see you at...' he paused for a second '...nine o'clock tomorrow morning.' That laugh came again. 'I thought I might need to work harder to persuade you.' His voice softened a little. 'I'm glad you have no other pressing cases. Because this family really do need you. *We* need you.'

'And I'm happy to be invited,' she said. 'Until tomorrow.'

He closed the call and Autumn collapsed backwards onto her bed. Had that really just happened?

It was like a dream. A fascinating surgery. A chance to visit a beautiful country and work with other people. Time to build a relationship with the parents of these girls and for them to trust what she could do. The real possibility that she could improve the overall outcome for these babies.

And Giovanni Lombardi had thought he might need to persuade her...

Now it was her turn to laugh out loud. She stared out of her window at the stars in the dark sky. 'What can I say, Giovanni? You had me at hello.'

CHAPTER TWO

HE WAS PACING. He knew he was pacing, and it was ridiculous.

Giovanni always started the day early, and Sofia was a morning person too, which was easy to manage. He also had some family assistance. Sofia's aunt was happy to take her to and from nursery, and to look after her for a few hours at either side.

All of this meant that by eight a.m. Giovanni was pacing in his office. He'd already met with Leon and Lizzy to discuss the Bianchi twins. He'd also reviewed the variety of other patients he currently had in the wards, and answered a number of specialist queries from around the world.

Steam was rising in the air from the coffee on his desk as he spotted a black limousine pulling up outside the hospital entrance. Unusual…

He watched as a woman with dark brown hair just past her shoulders emerged, wearing low heels, a black suit and a bright pink shirt. She gave her hair a shake and walked around to shake hands with the driver and exchange a few words with him. Both of them laughed and she gave him a wave.

She only had a small bag across her body and a small pull-along case at her feet. Four months. That was how long Autumn Fraser was supposed to be here. Had she changed her mind already? He'd expected her to arrive with numerous bags. This wasn't looking good.

His brain raced. He had agreed to all the demands she'd made before she arrived. He was sure he could agree to anything else that she asked for.

A few moments later he heard his PA's voice, and the door to his office opened.

Autumn Fraser glided into his office. She didn't look like a woman who, less than twelve hours ago, had been at home in London. Nor did she look like a woman who'd spent frantic hours packing and travelling, negotiating the confusing airport at Rome, then picking her way through an unfamiliar city.

He held out his hand to her. 'You've made good time, Dr Fraser. I'm impressed.'

She shot him a beaming smile as she pulled her case behind her, taking a quick glance around the room. Giovanni's office was spacious, with wide windows that allowed him a view of both the car park beneath and the beauty of the city around him.

'Not everyone arrives in a limousine,' he said, and kept smiling as he shook her hand. Her grip was firm and steady.

'I have some connections,' she said easily. 'When I travel, I like to concentrate on the case I'll be working on—not the hassle of the journey.' She gestured with her head to the large table on the other side of the office. 'Shall we sit there?'

Before he had a chance to reply, she'd moved over to the table and opened her pull-along case. He'd expected it to be full of clothes, but instead she pulled out her laptop and a mountain of research papers. Even from here he could see that she'd highlighted certain parts of them. Had she been up all night? And how could she possibly have worked like that on a plane?

Giovanni pressed his lips together. It was clear she didn't want to sit across a desk from him. Was this a power move, to make sure he knew they were on an equal footing?

As if she'd read his mind, she looked up at him from the desk, her green eyes serious. 'Let's start the way we mean to continue,' she said as she spread her papers across the table. 'I'd like to review the babies and talk techniques.'

She clearly worked exactly the same way as Giovanni—she liked to get straight to business—but for the first time in his career he decided to buck the trend.

'Actually, Dr Fraser—or would you prefer I call you Ms? Or Autumn?'

'Autumn will be fine.' Her response was automatic.

'Autumn, then. I'd like to show you around the hospital, make a few introductions, and then discuss the case. Once we've done that, I'll take you to meet the Bianchis. But first, before all that, I'm going to take you to breakfast.'

She blinked, looking momentarily stunned. She'd obviously expected him to get straight to work with her. And normally he would have. But Autumn Fraser wasn't what he'd expected. She didn't appear to be tired. Or nervous in any way. He could already see the work she'd done in the last few hours.

Maybe this woman just had a smooth veneer, or some glossy outer armour. But she had to be tired. And she had to be excited about this case. He'd told her he'd have to check she was a good fit—for him and the team. Her confident demeanour surprised him. But that was fine.

The thing that wasn't fine was how right Sofia had been. Autumn Fraser *was* pretty. More than pretty. Unnervingly pretty—in a way that she clearly didn't realise. From those startling green eyes to the wavy loose curls and tall, slender figure. He didn't know a single man on the planet who wouldn't look twice. It irked him that he topped that list. He wasn't used to distractions at work.

'I don't normally eat breakfast,' she said, with a wave of her hand.

Those green eyes connected with his. *Wow*. His breath caught somewhere at the back of his throat.

He raised his eyebrows. 'Hasn't anyone told you it's the most important meal of the day?'

He liked her. She was sassy. In a good way. He'd had that feeling last night when they'd talked on the phone.

She rolled her eyes, but stood up when he gestured to the door.

'You're right,' he said. 'Let's start the way we mean to continue. Let me take you for a traditional Italian breakfast.'

This was all going so wrong. All the way over on her comfortable flight she'd thought about that smooth voice on the phone. She hadn't let herself do an internet search for Giovanni Lombardi because she was hoping her fears wouldn't be answered. But here he was in the flesh. Mr Italian Gorgeousness. *Ugh*.

His broad shoulders and tailored suit, along with those dark flashing brown eyes and his easy manner, made him a combination of every Italian dreamboat she'd ever seen on screen. Even down to the short moustache and beard that didn't really resemble a beard. More like four or five days of deliberate not shaving. Italian men knew how to wear facial hair in such a sexy way...

This was so not what she needed right now. This was a career-making case. The last thing she wanted was any distractions.

She gulped. This was verging on a disaster for her, and her brain didn't normally have such thoughts. Less than twenty-four hours ago she'd been sitting at her friend's wedding with Louis by her side. They might have parted ways amicably, but in her head she'd believed she wouldn't even contemplate looking at another guy for months—at least not deliberately.

This surgery was far too important to allow herself to be distracted by anything—least of all thoughts about men. Long-term relationships had never been on her agenda. The example of her parents had planted that seed in her head a long time ago. Her mother had been a brilliant physicist. Her father an esteemed professor of history. Neither of them had seemed interested in parenting.

She wasn't quite sure how she and her brother had actually got into this world. It was as if academia had told her parents they should have a couple of kids, and so they'd dutifully ticked that box. But with an entire childhood of being pushed towards perfection, control and study, she'd never really learned to play, let alone love. Whilst other friends had considered marriage and a family, Autumn had never contemplated that for herself. She hadn't allowed herself to.

Her career focus was all-consuming. The last thing she wanted was a husband and children. It had always been clear to her that her parents had never achieved a balance between career and family life. She didn't want to be the same. So a husband and children were off the table, and every single thing about Giovanni Lombardi was sending her into panic mode.

She hadn't been joking when she'd said he'd had her at hello. That voice just sent electricity dancing over her skin. How could she do this job without a) looking at him, or b) listening to him? Switching off her senses seemed to be the only way to go, because he just oozed magnetism in a way it would be hard to ignore.

She couldn't remember ever having a reaction to a man like this.

And that was entirely the problem.

She stood, following him as he gestured with

his hand that they were to leave his office. Her brain tried to stay entirely focused on work. The hospital seemed impressive. On the outside, it looked like any grand old Italian building. But the inside was more akin to some kind of space-ship. The credentials she'd read on the website certainly showed that St Nicolino's had all the facilities she could need for this surgery and this case.

Giovanni tried to make small talk as they walked the long corridors. She was hoping he would take her to the impersonal hospital can-teen—but, no, he ushered her out through the main door and into a large four-by-four. Her eyes noticed the child booster seat in the back.

Moments later the car stopped outside a small café on the outskirts of Rome. The traffic had been heavy, but Giovanni had woven the large vehicle down narrow streets that had made her hold her breath.

Before she had a chance to think, he was out of the car and opening up the door for her. 'Here,' he said. 'My favourite place for break-fast.'

Autumn was interested. It wasn't flash, or chic. It looked exactly what it was: a small busi-ness in amongst a hundred others.

He put his fingers to his lips. 'Best coffee and best *maritozzo* in Rome.'

He kissed his fingers and blew into the air and she laughed out loud. 'Best *what*?'

He guided her inside, towards a glass cabinet stocked with food. 'Or, if you prefer, you can have a croissant, a *bombolone*, or *biscottate*.'

She was here for four months. She didn't doubt she'd try them all. 'I'll have what you're having,' she said. It seemed the simplest solution.

He nodded, and spoke in rapid Italian to the woman behind the counter. Listening to him talk his own language was magical. It took her a few moments to realise he was speaking to her again, asking her how she preferred her coffee.

A few minutes later they were sitting at a table outside. 'Your bags?' asked Giovanni. 'You have others?'

Autumn wrinkled her brow. 'I dropped them at my hotel on my way to the hospital.'

She could almost see his sigh of relief. He seemed to settle back into the slightly uncomfortable metal chair. She tried to hide her smile as she looked at the food on the table in front of her. Had he really thought she'd arrived with no luggage?

'You didn't want to catch a few hours' sleep or freshen up before coming to the hospital?' he asked, and then he seemed to realise how those words might sound and gave a slightly unnerved laugh. 'Sorry, I didn't mean it to sound like that.'

Autumn looked down at her old but still presentable clothes. They weren't rumpled. She gave him a direct stare. 'I showered on the plane and changed before I disembarked.'

There. Let him think that one over.

She could see the question form in his brain, but it never left his lips. *What kind of plane has a shower?*

'Actually,' she said as she took a sip of her coffee—*caffe macchiato*, coffee with a drop of milk, 'because you caught me at short notice, half my wardrobe was out of my reach. I might need you to get someone to direct me to a few places in Rome where I can pick up some more clothes.'

Now he looked even more surprised. 'You don't need someone else. I can do that.' He waved his hand easily.

'You shop for women's clothes?' she asked.

Autumn was staring at the *maritozzo* on the plate in front of her. It had turned out to be an Italian sweet pastry stuffed with cream and likely a million calories. There was no way she could eat that without getting it all over her.

Giovanni handed her a large cloth napkin as he tucked one into his shirt collar. He gave a careless shrug. 'All Italian men know where to shop,' he said simply.

She wasn't quite sure what to make of that,

and then she remembered the booster seat in the car. Her eyes went automatically to his left hand. No wedding ring was there.

But, like herself, Giovanni was a surgeon. There was a good chance he didn't wear a wedding ring. When scrubbing was a part of daily life, jewellery became a nuisance.

'I noticed the car seat,' she said, trying to say it as casually as possible. 'Do you have children?'

His eyes met hers and she would have sworn she saw them light up right before her.

He beamed. 'A daughter—Sofia. She's five and the light of my life.'

Everything about him changed in an instant. The tone of his voice, the relaxation of his shoulders. She'd thought he'd seemed quite easy around her already, but there was a visible difference now.

'Tell me about her.'

Autumn knew people. She'd been a doctor for years. This was a fellow surgeon she'd have to work alongside. It was essential that she knew what was important to him, and Sofia clearly was.

'She's fantastic. I may be biased, but I don't care. She's smart, but she likes to pretend she's not. She's already told me that being a surgeon is too boring and she plans to be an astronaut. She's always trying to learn something new, but…' He paused for a second. 'I imagine she'll do something completely different.'

'Why?'

Autumn was curious. She didn't have much experience with kids. Babies, yes. But, as sad as it sounded, when babies were in the neonatal unit there was a certain element of control. They could be monitored carefully, their medication adjusted. Comfort given. Feeding regimes measured as much as possible.

Of course things did sometimes go wrong, but with babies in one place and under her guidance she generally felt she could do as much as possible for the tiny, gorgeous, helpless little people. Once they got a bit older, and could move, walk, run, eat anything they found, they generally became the biggest safety hazard around and a heart attack waiting to happen. No. The complete randomness and unpredictability of them terrified her. So, she was interested. Could a parent really predict what their child might do when it was only aged five?

'She's a people person. Like a moth to a flame. Sofia loves people. All kinds of people— everywhere. I've never gone to a place with Sofia where she hasn't found a person to talk to. And she talks to them because she's interested. She wants to know everything about them.'

He gave a shrug.

'She's too young to realise just how important that is.' A frown creased his brow for a second. 'She's intuitive too. Seconds after she meets someone, she'll tell me if she likes them or not. At first, I used to laugh it off. Because we all do that. We all form first impressions. But…' He breathed out slowly. 'There have been a couple of occasions when she's been right and I've been wrong.' His dark eyes met Autumn's. 'Let's just say I've learned to pay attention.'

A car's horn sounded right next to them and they both jumped. Autumn squeezed the pastry she'd just lifted, causing a large dollop of cream to land on the plate. A moped darted between two cars, narrowly missing a pedestrian.

The traffic here was crazy. Thank goodness she'd made the decision not to drive. But the hotel she was staying at was a little way from the hospital. She'd have to ask Giovanni about public transport.

She toyed with the idea of sweeping up the piece of cream with her finger, but decided it was too impolite. Even though she'd never eaten something like this for breakfast before, her stomach was starting to rumble in anticipation.

'It sounds like you have a great relationship with your daughter,' she said.

'Of course—it's just me and her.'

He said the words simply, and she realised he'd probably had to say them a hundred times before.

She didn't need to ask. His wife hadn't left him. She knew that instantly.

'I'm sorry to hear that, Giovanni. But I'm sure Sofia has everything she needs in her obviously doting dad.'

He gave a sigh and leaned back in the chair. He glanced at the roads around them, wincing as a few more scooters seemed to take risky chances.

He lowered his voice. 'My wife died just before Sofia's first birthday. She was travelling to the hospital for an emergency. She was on a scooter and she was hit by a speeding driver.'

Autumn shivered. She couldn't help it. There had already been several near misses in the time they'd sat here. And the incident he'd just described... Things like that terrified her. Random, no reason, no control. She hated everything about those elements of the world outside her control.

As a medical student she'd taken some anti-anxiety medication for a time, and seen a counsellor to help her accept that there would always be things out of her control. It had taken four years, but she'd gradually accepted that. However, as soon as the counsellor had dug a little deeper about her feelings, repressed emotions and her upbringing, Autumn had stopped attending. She'd got what she needed to be able to function well enough in life.

But hearing stories like this always made her feel slightly panicky. One person's actions—a foot just a bit too heavy on the accelerator—had changed Giovanni and his daughter's life for ever. She'd always wondered how people coped after something like that.

'You must miss her.' It seemed the most obvious thing to say, and she didn't want him to see the tiny shake of her hands.

He gave a sad smile, his eyes looking a little darker than before. 'I'm sad that she's lost her part in Sofia's life. They were so alike. I think Anna would have got great joy from watching her grow every day. I also think they might have argued constantly...'

The smile grew warmer. He could obviously see them both in his head. But then he lifted his gaze again.

'But we can't live in the past. I have a duty to help Sofia live every day to the full. We talk about Anna, and I show her pictures, but I make sure her life is full of joy.'

Autumn could feel herself blinking back tears. *Wow.* This was the last thing she'd expected. But part of her was glad. She was glad she hadn't made a blunder and asked Giovanni about his wife. She was also glad that Giovanni was in a position where he felt as if he could share. He seemed sad, but not grief-stricken. A tiny, selfish part of her knew that meant he would be able to focus completely on their case.

As she watched Giovanni, he started to eat his pastry. He had the cloth napkin perfectly placed to catch any errant blobs of cream. It appeared he was an expert at *maritozzo*-eating. She took a few nervous bites herself, the burst of sweetness on her lips giving her an instant sugar rush.

She laughed. 'This can so *not* become a habit. Between the coffee and the sugar this morning, I will probably be jittery all day. Not to mention the pounds I could gain.'

He seemed back to his easy self, and the momentary shadows she'd seen flicker across his eyes had now vanished.

She glanced over at him, talking more before she thought. 'There's no way *you* do this every day!'

There wasn't a pick of fat on him. He was lean, but in a muscular kind of way. It was visible through his suit jacket, and the wicked smile he gave her in response made heat rush to her cheeks.

'Oh, sorry. That didn't quite come out how it should have.'

But now there was a cheeky glint in his eye, and she had to admit that she liked it.

'Maybe it came out exactly like it should have.' Giovanni glanced at his watch. 'Perhaps we should get back and I can give you the tour. Then we can get down to work.'

Autumn dabbed at the edge of her mouth with the napkin, praying she wasn't going back to her new place of work with cream on her face.

They jumped back in the car and Giovanni wove his way back to St Nicolino's.

Walking through the hospital with Giovanni was an enlightening experience. Everyone stopped to talk to him. She smiled as she remembered what he'd said about his daughter. Did he really not realise where she got her 'people person' traits from?

Giovanni reminded her of a paediatrician she'd worked with when she was a student. Dr Blair had remembered the name of every patient he'd ever seen. He'd been a wonderful mentor, and she'd lost hours of her life waiting while random strangers stopped him in the street, thanking him for looking after a relative years before. He'd remembered every case.

Walking with Giovanni was like walking the streets of her home town back in Scotland with Dr Blair.

She'd heard a mixture of languages around

her. She had been slightly worried, coming to Italy. Italian wasn't exactly a second language for her, although she could get by. But since setting foot in this hospital she had found most of the staff spoke English to her. It was a relief, but that didn't mean she wouldn't still make an effort to speak Italian.

St Nicolino's was a state-of-the-art hospital, and the sprawling tour wasn't for the fainthearted. She saw the wards and ICU, and the operating theatre complex, where Giovanni reassured her that her surgical privileges had been put in place for her. Then they toured the X-ray department, and met the sonogram and radiology staff. He showed her the changing facilities, the offices, where he introduced her to the admin assistants, then the overnight rooms and canteen facilities.

Then he led her down a quieter corridor and threw open the door to a wide room. 'This is where we'll spend most of our time.'

She blinked for a moment, trying to take in the sight in front of her. It was clearly a training room—a room where doctors at all stages of their career could practise and hone their clinical skills. She'd been in many rooms like this over the course of her career. But none had been quite like this one.

This room was full of tiny 3D-printed mannequins. Perfectly made tiny babies, all anatomically correct, and all at various points in surgery.

She frowned as she turned to Giovanni. 'You practise every surgery?'

Cost. That was the first thing that flew into her head. She'd often asked for a specific 3D mannequin to be built, to allow her to practise a surgery that she hadn't performed before. She knew exactly how much each of them would cost. But right now, the fact that here she'd have the chance to practice surgeries again and again was making her smile from ear to ear.

She'd methodically ticked off all the people she'd met and the places she'd been today on a list in her head. There were still a few key staff and facilities she'd have to discover. But this room… There was a real danger this would distract her completely.

Giovanni nodded. 'We have our own design team and 3D printing capabilities. They have already made mannequins of the Bianchi twins that Lizzy and Leon can practise on. The truth is, we don't know exactly when we might have to operate on these babies. We have to be prepared at any point in time. And, as you'll know, size plays a huge factor in these surgeries. Of course,' he continued, 'I hope we have many more weeks to prepare. But our team are performing weekly sonograms, and every time they do another, our modellers make us 3D mannequins of the twins. Sometimes multiple mannequins. The surgery that you and I will perform will be very different from the surgery Leon and Lizzy will likely have to do.'

Autumn gave a solemn nod as she moved over to one of the pairs of mannequins. This one was sealed in the amniotic sac. One of the babies would likely need cardiac surgery before delivery. The delicacy and precision of the operation would be absolutely crucial. Performing in utero surgery was a real skill. She didn't envy Lizzy and Leon their task.

The lighting in this room was as bright as in any theatre, and a whole host of tiny instruments was laid out on the tables at one side. She walked over, her eyes scanning along the trays, instantly looking for the tools she might need for her surgeries.

She hadn't even heard Giovanni move, so the low voice behind her made her jump. 'Just give me a list of what you need. You'll have it in days.'

She could feel his warm breath at the back of her neck. He was very near, obviously looking at the trays too.

She should step to one side. They were too close for comfort. But she pressed her lips together for a second and closed her eyes, taking a deep breath.

It was too soon. Too soon to consider anything. She'd never felt a pull like this before. It unnerved her. She was always the calmest person in the room. So why didn't she feel like that today?

'Most of what I need is here already. There might be a few specialist instruments. I'll give you a list later.'

Now she did step to the side and turn to face him. 'Can we meet the parents now?'

He gave the briefest nod of his head. 'Of course.'

As he turned towards the door again she let out her breath. The air-conditioning in the room kept its temperature steady. She just wished her body would do the same.

She was just tired. That was what it must be. She'd been running on adrenaline since his call last night. Because what she really didn't want to do right now was acknowledge the way her skin prickled and her heart-rate picked up any time she was around this man.

They had to work closely for the next few months. All her focus had to be on these babies. And Giovanni Lombardi was a distraction she *definitely* didn't need.

CHAPTER THREE

GIOVANNI LED HER to a large, comfortable room on the far side of the maternity unit. It was close enough to all emergency facilities without being in the middle of an impersonal ward.

He beamed as he walked into the room. 'Gabrielle, Matteo—I want you to meet Autumn Fraser. She's a specialist surgeon from Scotland.'

He turned towards Autumn as he moved to a comfortable sofa.

'Autumn, this is Gabrielle and Matteo Bianchi. Gabrielle is from Geneva, where they live, but they are staying with us. Matteo is from here, and has rented a villa in Rome, and Gabrielle is being monitored on a daily basis.'

Autumn could see the worry lines on the faces of both parents. They'd likely had the shock of their lives when they'd learned about their babies. The nerves and the strain were apparent even at first glance.

Autumn walked over to them, holding out her

hand to shake with each of them. 'It's a pleasure to meet you.' She knew how important it was to earn the trust of parents. And she was quite sure she would be every bit as anxious if she were in their shoes.

She sat next to Giovanni as he started talking again. 'I told you I was going to find a surgeon to lead the second team.' He put his hand on his chest. 'I'll be leading the team working with Hope, and Autumn will be leading the team working with Grace.'

Autumn's stomach gave a little flip. He'd mentioned this would be a trial agreement. But introducing Autumn as the surgeon leading the other team didn't seem like any kind of trial.

'The babies have names? That's fantastic,' she said. 'I love them.'

Gabrielle gave a nervous half-smile, her hands on her swollen stomach. She glanced at her husband. 'We did it a few weeks ago. We thought that if we gave them names now, it might bring us good luck.'

Autumn understood. Parents often had different opinions. She'd done other surgeries on conjoined twins where the teams had been called Twin A and Twin B. Some parents were terrified of naming babies who might not make it. They wanted to wait until they were actually born, then give them names.

Gabrielle and Matteo obviously wanted their daughters to be known by name from the beginning. Some people thought it might make their children more real. For them, as well as for others.

Giovanni gave a slow nod. Autumn knew he could have told her earlier, but it was clear he'd wanted to give the parents their place. She put her hand on her chest. 'So, I'll be in charge of Team Grace. I can promise you that we're going to plan for both your daughters carefully and do all we can to give them the best outcome possible.'

She could see Giovanni's sideways glance. It was always important in conversations like these that surgeons didn't promise they could save the babies. Autumn would have loved to do that. But these surgeries were filled with risks, as were the surgeries prior to separation. She could guarantee she would do everything she could for Team Grace, but anything else would be unethical.

Giovanni leaned forward. 'So, both myself and Autumn will talk you through all the aspects of the separation. But we don't want to overwhelm you. You know that Leon and Lizzy have to do their surgeries first? Once they have finished, we'll take over. But just know that we'll be working hard behind the scenes to get things ready for our surgeries after the Caesarean section.' He leaned forward and put his hand on Gabrielle's. 'One day at a time. Just know we're always here.'

Gabrielle blinked, unshed tears visible in her eyes. She gave a silent nod.

Giovanni stood up and Autumn joined him. 'Nice to meet you both,' she said. 'If you want to talk to me, just let one of the staff know and I'll be here.'

As they left the room Autumn could feel the weight of the meeting on her shoulders. Giovanni was walking alongside her, and his hand brushed against hers, drawing her attention. The buzz going up her arm was instant and undeniable.

'The first introduction is always the toughest. I'm trying to give them space to process everything without overwhelming them. Lizzy and Leon are their primary caregivers right now.'

She raised her eyebrows, sure that it must be driving him crazy, and he nodded.

'Yep, I find it difficult not to constantly check things. But I have a short meeting first thing every morning with Lizzy and Leon, then I drop in to see the parents at some point during the day.'

'You need them to have faith in Leon and Lizzy.'

'Absolutely. We'll take over when we need to.'

He stopped for a moment and leaned on a railing to look out over the wide entrance and the floors beneath them. 'This is one of the most complicated cases we've ever had.'

Autumn joined him, leaning down and looking at the bustling hospital. She could see the sigh of absolute relief from everyone who walked through the front doors, out of the searing heat of Rome and into the air-conditioned space inside the hospital. She shivered, not sure if it was caused by the temperature around her, the man next to her, or the huge pressures of the surgery ahead.

'Do you have a gestation in mind that you think we'll need to work to?'

He nodded. 'I'm approximating around thirty-two weeks right now. Lizzy and Leon's surgery will be soon. From there, it just depends on how Gabrielle and the babies do after that. We could require immediate delivery, or we might manage a reasonable amount of time after that.'

Autumn nodded. Everyone knew that babies tended to do better the closer to normal gestation they were delivered. Most twins these days were delivered before forty weeks. These babies would never last to that point. But thirty-two weeks wasn't unreasonable. If things went well, both babies might be able to breathe with minimum assistance at that stage, and would also have the ability to suck, swallow and feed. Every baby was an individual, and they wouldn't really know until the twins were here, but thirty-two weeks was something to aim for.

She turned to face Giovanni. 'So, we're likely have a maximum of seven weeks to prepare for this surgery?'

Part of her body was going into panic mode. The intricacies of her liver surgery were going to be more than difficult. The separation between Hope and Grace would be tricky enough, and once that was done she would literally have to build Grace a liver, hoping she could also sort out an adequate blood supply.

'Are you okay?'

Giovanni moved quickly, his hand on her arm, and she caught the woody scent of his aftershave.

'Fine,' she said quickly. She wanted to start practising right this second. But she knew it was a bad idea.

Giovanni's fingertips on her arm pressed gently. 'How about an early dinner? I know a five-year-old who would love to meet you.'

She hesitated. She wanted to get back to her hotel room, lie down on the giant bed and just let it swallow her whole. Processing...there was so much processing her brain had to do right now.

'Sofia wants to meet me?' she asked.

One eyebrow flicked upwards. 'She picked you.'

'What?' His words came as a complete surprise and left her momentarily stunned.

He gave a serious nod as he steered her down the corridor again. 'Truthfully. She looked at all the faces I had on my computer screen and told me to pick you.'

Autumn's skin prickled in annoyance. 'I hope you're joking.'

Giovanni shrugged. 'Let's just say you were already joint top of the list anyway.'

Autumn stopped walking. *Joint?* She couldn't keep the indignation out of her voice. 'Who did you think matched me?'

He named another surgeon from the US, who specialised in paediatric liver surgery. She wasn't quite so offended, but still annoyed.

'I'm better than him...'

He opened the door to the office he'd shown her earlier, where her bag and jacket were stored. 'It was your studies into the psychological trauma of separation that swayed me.'

She'd just bent to pick up her bag and stopped dead. 'Really? You know about that?' That was another surprise. Most fellow surgeons just looked at her skill set and success rate. They didn't look into the other aspects of medicine she'd explored.

He nodded as he moved towards her. 'I've read your papers. I like your concepts. I don't have your depth of knowledge, but I've often wondered about the trauma of separation for conjoined twins. And I don't mean the physical trauma.'

Her mouth was dry. 'You believe there's a psychological side?'

She'd met other scholars who wouldn't be convinced about the principle of psychological trauma for neonates. It was almost a relief to find someone who believed in it and was interested to learn more. Too many other surgeons just wanted to talk about clinical procedures and techniques.

'Of course I believe it.' His husky voice revealed no doubt.

She could have sworn some magical creature had just run down the length of her spine.

Giovanni tilted his elbow towards her. 'Let's pick up Sofia and go for dinner. I'll drop you back at your hotel afterwards.'

'You don't mind eating early?' She knew Italians were known for their late dinners.

He shook his head. 'I have a five-year-old who I like to get to bed at a reasonable time. Believe me, Sofia needs no excuse to be up half the night.'

Autumn hesitated. She was tired, but she had to eat, and she still hadn't planned how to travel to and from the hospital. She gave a slow nod. 'Thanks,' she said, then added, 'I'd love to meet Sofia. Just to let her know that I'm truly the best candidate.'

She gave him a straight-eyed stare and he laughed.

As they walked out to the car park she wrinkled her nose. 'When you spoke to me yesterday, you said you had to make sure I was a good fit for the team. I'm assuming that as you've introduced me to the parents, you think that I am?'

He held the car door open for her for the second time today. There was a gleam in his eye. 'I might,' he said, 'but you still have to pass the final hurdle.'

'What's that?'

'Sofia,' he said, and grinned as he closed the door and walked around to the other side.

Giovanni could tell from the expression on her face that Autumn hadn't worked out yet that he was toying with her.

He went in to pick up Sofia and she dashed straight out to the car as soon as she knew who was in it. He hadn't even managed to collect her bag and jacket before she'd climbed into the car and started to fasten her seatbelt, the whole time talking constantly.

'You're Autumn? Do you know that's a season? I had to look it up. I'm Sofia. I'm five. How long will you work with my *papà*? Are you staying with us?' She started to bounce a little in her car seat, even though she was strapped in.

Giovanni slid into the car and gave Autumn a grin. 'Sofia, calm down. Wait until we're at the restaurant before you start asking questions.'

Autumn looked dumbstruck. 'Her English is amazing. Much better than my Italian.'

He nodded, the feeling of pride making his chest swell. 'Yes, her English is good. Obviously. As is her Italian. She can also speak a little Greek and a little Japanese. She attends an international school and she seems to pick up languages...' he wrinkled his nose for a second '...how do you say it? Like a sponge?'

Giovanni pulled away and moved into the traffic. It was busy. There was much horn-sounding, gesturing and shouting. It seemed that Giovanni wasn't shy about shouting either.

He let out a yell as someone cut in front of them and Sofia started laughing. Her laugh was light. But Autumn was gripping the sides of the seat. She'd heard about the traffic in Rome, but she'd never experienced it first-hand. She glanced sideways at Giovanni, wondering how it felt to drive in this every day, knowing that his wife had died in a traffic accident.

She literally felt as if an accident could happen around about them at any second. But Sofia didn't seem upset or worried. She was young… This was likely her everyday normal.

Around ten minutes later Giovanni pulled up in an older part of the city. As Autumn climbed out of the car, she pulled the damp hair from the back of her neck. The journey hadn't been quite what she'd expected. Stopping was a complete and utter relief.

Sofia jumped out and ran into the restaurant. Autumn turned and smiled wearily at Giovanni. 'Come here often?'

He let out a low laugh. 'Perhaps. Watch out or she'll order for you.'

As they walked inside, it was clear that this was a restaurant owned by his friends. Sofia had settled herself at a booth and was tapping the top of the table for them both to join her. 'Autumn, sit next to me,' she said.

Giovanni slid into the seat across from her. 'What am I? Old news?' he asked. But from the way he was grinning Autumn could tell he wasn't offended.

An older woman appeared, kissing Giovanni

on both cheeks and putting some water and glasses on the table. She turned and said something in rapid Italian to Autumn, but Giovanni shook his head, clearly explaining that Autumn wouldn't understand.

He pointed to the water. 'Would you prefer some wine with dinner?' he asked.

She shook her head. She was already exhausted, and her head was so full. She felt as if even a sip of wine would knock her out. 'Water's great, thanks.'

The older woman switched easily to English, and spoke between two languages as she took their orders.

'Which is best?' Autumn asked Sofia, pointing at a few items on the menu, who then took great delight in deciding on her order.

Ten minutes later she had a delicious plate of rigatoni in front of her, in a creamy tomato sauce with bacon through it, along with a heap of garlic bread in a basket between them all. It was hitting all the right spots.

She'd also answered what seemed like a million questions from Sofia, who was currently tucking in to her dinner. Autumn smiled. Both Giovanni and Sofia had their cloth napkins tucked into their collars. Cute.

Giovanni glanced at Sofia. 'It's the only time

she's quiet,' he said jokingly. 'Take advantage while you can.'

Autumn shook her head and looked at him steadily. 'She's a delight.'

She could see the pleasure in his eyes. He glanced back at his daughter and she could almost feel the strength of his love for her stretching across the table to grab her.

Sofia wasn't quite so terrifying as she'd feared a child might be. Drinks hadn't been spilled yet, nor dinner dropped on clothes—in fact, if anyone was going to do that, it was much more likely to be Autumn. She was struggling to keep her eyes open.

Her brain started drifting. Father and daughter seemed so easy around each other... She wondered if he ever got strict with her at home or if he was always like this.

It wasn't as if she knew anything about bringing up a child. Sure, Autumn had friends with children. She'd even offered to take a good friend's baby overnight, when her friend had started to look as if she might blow away in a puff of wind. She'd taken the baby back at lunchtime the next day and smiled sweetly, not admitting that she'd been up all night, terrified, watching the rise and fall of her friend's sweet son's chest.

She often stayed late in the ICU units at the

hospitals she worked in in London. It was comforting, holding a baby against her chest, rubbing its back gently to settle it, all the while knowing she could be surrounded by ten people at a moment's notice.

It was easy being confident with tiny babies in a hospital. She didn't imagine for a single second it was easy being home alone in charge of a tiny person. And as Autumn watched Giovanni she couldn't pretend she didn't admire him right now. Sofia was a lovely kid—bright, fun and well-mannered.

'You okay?' he asked softly.

She gave a little start, embarrassed to have been caught staring.

'Just tired,' she said, pushing her plate away. 'The food here is delicious. I'll need to remember how to get here.'

A small hand landed on her arm. 'You can't come here without me.' Sofia's wide eyes were serious. 'I need to tell Mamma Pieroni what you want.'

Autumn put her hand over Sofia's. 'Well, I'll tell you what—next time I want to come I'll let your dad know and he can see if you're free.'

For a second Sofia's brow creased, as if she were an adult contemplating something, and then her face lit up in a smile again. 'Okay, then.'

Giovanni had slid from his seat and moved

away whilst she was talking to Sofia. He strolled back over. 'Sofia, it's time to go home. We need to drop Autumn back at her hotel. She's had a long day and she is very tired.'

Autumn realised distractedly that Giovanni must have settled the bill. 'Sorry,' she said quickly as she fumbled for her bag. 'Let me pay. I didn't expect you to buy me dinner.'

His reply was as quick as lightning and in a joking tone. 'But remember this wasn't dinner. This was a test.'

She sighed as she wriggled out of the booth. 'Then please tell me that I passed.'

As she slid into the car, she noticed what looked like a bus stop on the other side of the road. 'Oh, can you tell me the best way to get to the hospital from my hotel? Should I use the bus, the tram, or the metro?'

'None,' he said as he clicked his seatbelt into place. 'I'll pick you up.'

'You can't do that,' she said automatically. 'I don't want to put you to any trouble. Particularly when you have Sofia to think of.'

'It's no trouble.' His voice was smooth.

Autumn shook her head again. 'No, it would be a complete imposition. And I need to learn to find my way around the city by myself.'

The car eased into the traffic and Giovanni gave a nonchalant shake of his head. 'Maybe in a few days. But I'll pick you up for the next few mornings. Point out a few other places to you and give you some time to find your feet.'

He made himself sound like some kind of tour guide… It wasn't that she didn't appreciate the offer—of course she did. But Autumn had always been an independent woman. She might not contemplate driving a car in the complicated system around her, but she definitely wanted to be mobile on her own.

'It's a kind thought,' she said firmly, 'but I like to find my own way.'

There was a tiny crease in his brow. If she hadn't been so tired, she might have been amused. She wasn't sure if it was Italian chivalry or a colleague being protective, but relying on Giovanni to get her to and from work was a definite no-no.

They would be working closely enough already. It hadn't even been a whole day and already she was trying to pretend she didn't find this man attractive, compelling, intelligent and incredibly sexy. She'd definitely need some space to allow her senses a chance to recover.

Now, even though she could sense the tiniest hint of annoyance, he gave a nod of his head. 'How about we just settle on me collecting you tomorrow morning and I'll show you where the transport links are on the way to the hospital?

There are a few places I'd warn you to avoid so you can stay safe.'

'Tomorrow morning,' Autumn repeated, with a reluctant nod of her head.

She was watching the fascinating attractions and the streets of Rome stream past, and knew that she would want a chance to explore this city herself.

She turned to him and kept her voice firm. 'And then I'll be able to suit myself.'

There was an edge to her voice. She was drawing a line in the sand. Sofia was singing quietly in the seat in the back and Autumn didn't want to get into a fight with Giovanni.

There was a hint of a smile on his face. 'No problem,' he said, his accent thick.

He pulled his car up in front of her hotel and she let out a long, slow breath. She turned and smiled at Sofia. 'It was a pleasure to meet you, Sofia, and I hope we can meet again soon.'

Sofia stared at her with wide brown eyes. There were a few seconds of silence before the little girl gave a nod of her head. 'I think we're going to be friends,' she said solemnly.

Autumn smiled. 'I think so too.'

The door next to her clicked. She hadn't even realised Giovanni had slipped out of the car and opened her door for her. It seemed to be a habit of his.

She swung her legs out of the car, immediately swamped by the warm evening Rome air. As she stood up she stumbled a little, causing Giovanni to quickly slide an arm around her back.

'Okay?' he asked.

She turned her head—and froze. They were literally inches apart, and her body had decided to let her stop breathing. It was a close-up she hadn't imagined having.

His dark eyes seemed to pull her in. The remains of his aftershave drifted around her. His jacket was in her hands, and she was conscious of his warm fingers at her waist, their heat drifting through to her skin.

It was like being stopped in time. The noise of the city was there, but it seemed they were stuck in an imaginary bubble around them. Her eyes took in every part of his face. His dark hair, the short stubble of his beard and moustache, the tiny lines around the corners of his eyes…

'Did I pass the test?' she asked, in a voice so low she could barely hear herself.

His face creased into a smile. 'Always,' was his reply.

There was an instant of stillness between them, and then he dropped his arm and walked away.

Now she breathed. Sucking in the exhaust fumes of the others' cars around them. Numerous people were being dropped at the hotel. It wasn't as big as some of the others, but was obviously popular.

The noise around her seemed to amplify and she gave herself a shake. What *was* that? What had just happened?

'Seven o'clock tomorrow morning?'

Her head jerked up. Giovanni was at the other side of the car, ready to get back in.

She nodded her head. 'Absolutely—thank you.' She gave a wave to Sofia and headed to the hotel entrance.

A good night's sleep. That was all she needed. She'd been living on adrenaline since last night's telephone call. Today had been an overload. And she'd expected that...but not quite in the way it had occurred.

She walked through Reception and pressed the button for the lift. She would be fine. She would unpack the luggage she'd dropped earlier, shower, and drop straight into bed.

But even as she stepped into the lift her stomach gave a little twist. She already knew the face that would invade her dreams tonight...

CHAPTER FOUR

'WHAT'S WRONG, PAPÀ?'

Giovanni was staring out of the window, his head somewhere in the clouds. Sofia's voice jerked him back to attention and he finished buttoning the short-sleeved shirt he'd chosen to wear for work that morning.

'Nothing, darling,' he said quickly. 'I'll be ready in a moment.'

Sofia climbed up on to the chair next to him and gave him a hard stare. 'You keep doing that,' she said, a determined edge to her voice.

He tried not to smile. Sometimes Sofia acted like the adult in the household. Keeping Giovanni in line seemed to be her first priority.

He knelt down beside her. 'I keep doing what?'

'That thing.' She folded her arms across her chest.

'What thing?'

'The staring thing. Not paying attention.'

'To you?' The thought struck a pang through his heart.

'To everything.' She shrugged her shoulders, emphasising her folded arms.

Giovanni ran his hand through her hair. 'Sofia, you'll always be the centre of my attention. Sometimes Papà has to think about other things—work. But you always come first.'

'I know that,' she said in a small voice.

Giovanni held out his hand. 'Come on, then, let's get going.'

Sofia's hand slipped into his and he gave it a squeeze. He chatted easily until he dropped her off, then spent the rest of the way to the hospital swamped with guilt.

Called out by a five-year-old—and rightly so.

He'd been thinking about Autumn Fraser.

Ridiculous. One week. That was how long they'd been working together. His brain was constantly on overload, thinking about the intricate planning for the surgery. He couldn't spare any space—none at all—so he couldn't understand for a second why he continually found himself lost in thoughts about Autumn Fraser.

Of course, she was smart. Of course, she was unintentionally gorgeous. She definitely struggled with the language, but she was trying hard. He'd watched from the end of the corridor yesterday as she'd tried chatting to one of the domestic staff. Carla had been greatly amused with the new doctor trying out her Italian. But all of that was entirely superficial.

Giovanni knew that Autumn was here on a temporary basis. But from their first phone conversation he'd had a good feeling about her. This week she'd started to assess the staff around her as to their suitability for her team. She was pleasant to people, but had already revealed there were a few staff she was unsure of. He liked her honesty.

There had been no further breakfasts or dinners. She'd started taking the tram to work, and told him she was thoroughly enjoying the journey. But her office was right next to his. They spoke to each other every day. She'd started to accompany him on short visits to Matteo and Gabrielle.

'Giovanni?'

And there she was. Dressed in a pair of red scrubs.

He closed his laptop and moved over to join her, picking up his surgical cap as he headed to join her.

'Are you ready?'

He saw her hands were twisting together as they walked. He was dressed in his traditional navy scrubs and waved his hands down at his clothes. 'Do I look ready?'

'Oh, come on.' She nudged him as they headed to the clinical lab room, deliberately knocking him off his stride.

This was to be their first practice surgery. Of course, he was nervous.

Autumn kept talking. 'I'm worried about getting the positioning correct. I'm not sure I'll be able to reach the part of the liver I need to.'

She pulled her own surgical hat from her pocket as they opened the door to the lab. It was cream and covered in small red hearts. She tied up her hair and tucked the brown strands under her cap.

They'd both agreed to take this seriously. No one else was here for this first practice session. Autumn had seemed anxious to get started and had been impatient for their model to be ready. He wasn't quite sure if she was intimidated by this surgery—that would worry him—or just a control freak.

Giovanni mirrored her actions and tucked his hair under his own surgical cap. It had a little anchor at the front. It was like a ritual. He didn't know a single surgeon who didn't have their own cap.

Autumn stared at him for a few moments with those big green eyes. She gave a nod of her head. 'You tell me about yours; I'll tell you about mine.'

Her Scottish accent seemed a little thicker, making the words all run together. It took him a few seconds to work out what she'd said.

Then he laughed. 'My dad was in the navy. When I told him about surgeons' hats, he produced this one a few days later.' He reached up and touched the cap again. 'He bought me a whole supply. Told me it was in case he wasn't around to see me wear them.'

Autumn tilted her head to one side. He could tell she understood without him having to say the words out loud. 'How long since you lost him?'

He gave a brief nod. 'Two years. He had cardiovascular disease. I'm just glad he got to meet Sofia. He was her biggest fan.' His fingers brushed his cap again, and visions of Sofia giggling on his father's lap played in his head.

He took a deep breath then, looked back at Autumn's cap. 'What about you with the love hearts?'

She shrugged. 'I lost a bet.'

'What?'

Autumn nodded. 'I don't need to tell you that surgery can be a pretty sexist area to work in. Most of the female surgeons I've worked under were power houses. One day me, and my fellow trainee surgeons, were talking about how most surgeons have a signature look, and contemplating what we'd choose if we made it through our programmes. One of the theatre assistants used to make caps for some of the staff. She had a ritual with trainees where she made what she thought suited them, laid out the caps and waited to see if they picked the right one.'

Giovanni was intrigued. He'd never heard anything like this before, but could imagine it taking place. 'So…?' he prompted.

'So, we came in one morning and there was a whole host of caps.' She counted off on her fingers. 'There were a few dark colours—some with motifs, like yours, or different patterns. There was one with bright yellow sunflowers, a green hat with a mountain range on it, another made of material that looked like the sea, one with rainbows, one with flames, and one with hearts.'

He wrinkled his nose. 'So how did you lose the bet?'

She waved her hand. 'Oh, we had to put our hand in a bag and pull out a number. I was last.'

'So you lost a lottery, not a bet?'

She smiled. 'You're being technical.'

Giovanni leaned against the surgical table he was next to. 'What would you have picked if you'd been first?'

She wrinkled her nose. 'I'm not sure. Probably leaves, because of my name.'

'But you got stuck with the hearts?'

She laughed and tucked another piece of hair under her cap. 'I did. And they've kind of stuck with me. Sometimes I imagine I want something crazy, like a unicorn or a space scene. But then I just revert back to my hearts.'

There was a gleam in Giovanni's eyes. 'Maybe you should switch to a liver.'

She gave him a gentle shove. 'Oh, very funny.' The last piece of hair disappeared and she stared at him. 'You know what turned out kind of nice? Avril—that's the theatre tech who made the caps— told me some time later that she'd meant the hearts for me anyhow.'

'She had?'

Autumn paused for a second, as if she was contemplating how she'd reply. Finally, she gave a nod of her head. 'Apparently I keep my heart close to my chest.'

Giovanni frowned and shook his head, not quite getting what she meant.

Autumn laughed. 'Sorry. It's a play on a figure of speech. You might have heard of keeping your cards close to your chest?'

'Ah, yes.'

'Well, she told me I keep my heart close to my chest. I'm careful. And she was right. I do. I am. I've always been like that. She read me better than I expected her to.'

Every part of him was curious. Did Autumn have a reason to be guarded with her heart? It suddenly struck him that she hadn't even mentioned anyone back home. He'd made an assumption that she was single. But he didn't actually know that. For some reason, he knew he absolutely had to find out.

He chose his words carefully, but kept his tone light. 'So, do you still keep your heart close to your chest, or have you already lost it to someone?'

She gave him a curious stare, and he cringed at how forward his question seemed. She wavered. She didn't answer straight away. And all of a sudden the lurch of his stomach was so much more important than how cringeworthy his question had been.

She let out a long slow breath. 'I just…' she paused and chose her words carefully '…parted company with someone.' Autumn gave a hollow laugh. 'I didn't even have time to move out properly. I paid a company to go and pack up my things and drop them at my flat.'

Now Giovanni leaned back further on the trolley and folded his arms across his chest. He laughed too. 'Is it just me—or does that seem harsh?'

Her cheeks flooded with colour and she lifted her hands to them automatically. She let out a groan. 'It does, doesn't it?' She kept her eyes closed for a second. 'He's a nice guy. I like him—I do. I just had a moment when I realised he wasn't right for me.' She wrapped her arms around herself, as if she was trying to give herself some comfort, then opened her eyes and shook her head. 'No, that's not it. We *both* had a moment when we realised we didn't have that thing.'

Giovanni raised his eyebrows. 'That thing…?'

He couldn't believe how easily they were talking to each other. It seemed as though they'd tiptoed around each other for the last few days. Not awkward, exactly, just never really alone and talking. At least not like this.

She smiled and sighed. 'Don't start with me. You know that thing. The thing that quickens your heart and sets your skin on fire.'

She was staring straight at him. He unfolded his arms from across his chest and took a step towards her. The model they would be practising on was lying on a theatre trolley between them.

His voice dropped an octave lower. 'When your mouth goes dry and your brain won't focus?'

Recognition flashed across her eyes. He saw she was surprised. Her words had been easy, as if she'd been relaxed and with her guard down.

But now she looked like a deer caught in the headlights.

As he watched she slowly licked her bottom lip. 'I guess...' It came out like a whisper. 'I'm not sure I've ever really experienced that. I'm not sure that I'll ever lose my heart to someone.' She gave a forced laugh. 'Anyway, we all know how important a heart is. It's too important an organ to lose.'

Giovanni took another step and laid his hands on his side of the trolley. She was trying to make light of those last words, but they hadn't gone unnoticed. He could ask more questions, but it probably wasn't the right time or the right place. So he took the easy way out. 'Then it sounds like you were right.'

Her head tilted slightly to the side. 'Right?'

'To walk away. Part as friends.'

She blinked. 'Of course. I'll always be his friend.'

Something lanced into Giovanni's heart. *Friends*. He hadn't told Autumn—or anyone—the truth about himself and Anna. Only a few short months after their daughter's arrival they'd been far from friends. The day she died she'd just launched a tirade at him before heading out on her scooter to go to work.

He'd told her she was still officially on leave. He'd been worried about her mental health after the birth of their daughter. A friend had been due to visit in a few days and assess her. Her behaviour had become, on occasion, increasingly erratic, with her flaring up out of nowhere. Other times she was calm and happy, but also a little restless.

Anna had always been like a butterfly, beating her wings against a window in a fight to get free. In the end, the last thing they'd been was friends, but he'd never shared that with anyone. Now, he was envious of the sad look in Autumn's eyes. She was sincere. She had genuinely parted from her ex as friends, and clearly wished him the best.

Her warm hand touched his arm. 'Giovanni? Are you okay?'

He jerked and looked up, putting a smile on his face. 'Oh, yes—sorry. Lost in my thoughts for a second.'

Her voice was soft. 'Thoughts about surgery, or thoughts about something else?'

Those green eyes were staring straight at him. She knew he hadn't been thinking about surgery and she was giving him an opening if he wanted it. But he couldn't. He couldn't share. Autumn was still almost a stranger, even though she didn't really feel like that.

He kept the smile on his face, knowing exactly how frozen it looked. Her gaze was steady.

Almost as if she were peeling back his layers to see exactly what was there.

He looked downwards at the model of the babies beneath them. There was so much work to do. So little preparation time. He couldn't allow his thoughts to wander elsewhere. They both had a duty and a responsibility to Hope and Grace.

He cleared his throat loudly. 'I think we should get to work.'

If Autumn was offended by his change in tone and conversation she was professional enough not to let it show. 'Of course.'

She could feel the awkwardness in the air, but refused to acknowledge it or let it put her off her game. She was here to do a job.

They'd spent the last four hours talking technique as they worked. The surgical instruments they were using were understandably tiny. Steady hands were crucial. As was correct positioning. In an ideal world, they would be working on opposite sides. But surgery like this was never ideal.

'I need access to the renal vein,' she said in a low voice, as Giovanni worked on the side across from her. His dark eyes looked up. 'Come on over,' he said, clearly concentrating on what he was doing.

Autumn nodded and moved around. His large

frame was bent over the models. His muscular arms held them in place. She dodged behind him, trying to find the best way to gain access.

'Problem?'

She hesitated. 'I may need to get a little closer.'

'Fine by me,' was the quick reply.

Her heart skipped a beat as she brushed up against his thin scrubs before ducking down and coming up between his arms. Her back was tight against his chest. One of her arms was intertwined with his, the other almost parallel. She shifted again, to allow her the optimum position to gain the access she would require.

She could feel the heat of his entire body, every bump, every ridge, against her spine.

Giovanni let out a low laugh. She felt his chest reverberate against her back.

'Sorry,' she whispered as she moved her hands delicately. 'But this is the only way to get access.'

His breath was at her neck and she knew he was watching her actions over her shoulder. 'It's a little up close and personal,' he whispered. 'But in the name of surgery I think we can sacrifice some personal space.'

There was laughter in his words and it made her tense muscles relax a little. With precision surgery there would always be an amount of tension. That was good. But too much tension could cause cramps and other problems. Truth was, this felt better than it should.

She didn't want to think about what she'd revealed earlier, and she hoped he hadn't picked up on it. The only person who'd caused her heart to race was this guy, the man she'd met just over a week ago.

She pushed back against him as she optimised her position in order to carry out the procedure she needed to.

He gave a little grunt and her stomach muscles clenched. Okay, this was maybe a bit *too* personal. She tilted her head, focusing, ignoring the rise and fall of the chest behind her. Another tiny clip and a positioning movement, to ensure the safety of the vein prior to separation... There— finally, she'd got it.

'Perfect.'

His voice was in her ear as she breathed a sigh of relief. Her muscles relaxed and she sagged back against him for a second.

'Wow,' she said.

But Giovanni didn't move. His hands remained entirely steady, locked in place to enable him to carry out the next part of the procedure once she was finished.

It took Autumn a few moments to realise what she was doing. She was comfortable leaning into him, feeling the heat of him through their thin scrubs and the relief of the procedure being over.

Then her brain kicked into gear. She gave a nervous laugh. 'Guess I'd better move,' she whispered as she ducked down through his arms. Her head ran along the length of his thigh. He gave a cough and she flinched away, continuing to laugh nervously.

It felt strangely sad to move away from him. Which was ridiculous. She'd only known him for a week.

She watched without talking as Giovanni finished his part of the procedure, then straightened up, stretching his back and taking a deep breath.

As he pulled his head straight again, he gave her a wide grin, a hint of amusement in his eyes. 'I guess we'd better get used to that.'

'What?' she asked, praying her face wasn't as flushed as it felt.

'Getting up close and personal,' he quipped, his accent seeming a little thicker than normal. 'We might end up in all sorts of positions.' He paused for a moment, as her face definitely did a full flush, then added, 'In order to complete the surgery.'

One eyebrow gave the tiniest arch as he finished the last words. Deliberate. He'd done that deliberately. She didn't know whether to laugh out loud or throw something. So she pulled her cap from her head and shook out her hair, letting it cover her face momentarily.

It was hot in here. Too hot. Did the air-conditioning need turning up, or was it just her?

Through her hair she looked down at the model again, trying her best to concentrate on the matter at hand. But it was hard. Her head was still swimming at the feel of Giovanni at her back, the sensation of his breath on the back of her neck, and the effect his voice had had on her.

She didn't do this. Not ever. She'd never experienced such an intense reaction to someone before and it all seemed so wrong. She was here to focus on two little girls.

'Let's do lunch,' said Giovanni, his words cutting through her thoughts.

Her mind went instantly to the nice dim restaurant he'd taken her to the time before. That was so *not* what she needed right now.

'I'm not sure that's a good idea.' The words came out before she had much time to think. She knew immediately they didn't sound quite right.

He stared at her, all humour lost. 'In the hospital canteen,' he said steadily, 'with a few of our potential colleagues for our teams. Let's brief them on how our first practice surgery went this morning, and how we would like to proceed.'

Embarrassment washed over her. He hadn't meant the two of *them*, specifically. Oh, no. His voice had a clipped edge, as if he were spelling things out to her exactly.

Giovanni had been welcoming and friendly when she'd arrived. Of course he had. Any surgeon would be. It was natural to pull out all the stops to entice another surgeon to stay if you wanted them to work alongside the team.

But she'd read too much into it.

She pulled her hair back. 'Of...of course. Of course. Give me ten minutes to freshen up. I'll meet you there.'

She was out through the door like a flash, her legs taking her rapidly down to the locker room. She flung open the door and leaned against the wall, her cap clutched in her hand. Within a few seconds she leaned over with her hands on her knees, groaning.

'Something up?' said an easy voice from the corner.

Darn it. She'd thought she was alone. Autumn snapped her head back up, ready to make some random excuses. But then her brain kicked in. The voice had spoken in English—not Italian. Lizzy Beckley was pulling on a pair of socks, sitting on a bench near the back of the room.

Autumn's shoulders sagged in relief. She tried to find words, but Lizzy gave her a knowing smile. 'That's the face of a woman who's been annoyed by an Italian man.'

Autumn took a few steps and sat down on the bench opposite her. 'You recognise it?'

They'd only met a few times, and had never had a chance to catch up properly, but she'd got a definite vibe of something weird between Lizzy and her Italian colleague Leon. What was more, it didn't seem to be on a professional basis...it seemed much more personal. From her rounded stomach, it looked as if Lizzy was pregnant, but Autumn didn't like to ask too many questions.

Lizzy nodded as she pushed her feet into her shoes. 'Oh, I know it well.'

She gave a little sigh as she picked up her bag and stood up. 'How about we talk some time? Is next week okay? I think us girls have to stick together.'

Autumn nodded. 'That would be perfect.'

She felt a wash of instant relief. They might not know each other well, but that recognition from another female who was likely in a similar position to herself was more than a bit welcome right now.

Lizzy put her hand on Autumn's shoulder as she walked past. 'We'll arrange a coffee next week. Hopefully away from this place.'

Autumn gave a grateful nod. Her eyes fell again to Lizzy's stomach as she watched her walk to the door, and Lizzy gave a little nod and rested her hands on her abdomen.

'How are you doing?' asked Autumn, keeping her words light and hoping they didn't sound intrusive.

'Eating for two.' Lizzy winked at her as she elbowed the door and walked out.

Interesting… The jungle drums were already talking about Leon and Lizzy. But Lizzy seemed remarkably cool about everything. How on earth was she feeling?

Autumn shook her head as she stood up again and pulled her scrubs from her body. She was slightly sticky, so she pulled her hair up on her head, grabbed new scrubs and headed to the staff showers. All the while wondering if Lizzy was as freaked out at the thought of having a child as Autumn knew *she* would be.

Giovanni wasn't entirely sure what he'd done wrong. Yes, they'd been up close and very personal. But, whilst it might not have been ideal, this type of surgery always carried that risk. Last time around, he and a male colleague had practically been breathing the same air in their attempt to position themselves appropriately for the sake of the separation surgery—and that one had been much less complicated than this.

Maybe it had been so long since he'd been that close to a woman that his senses were entirely off, but he could have sworn that when she'd finished her procedure Autumn had leant back into him, comfortably, for a few moments. She'd appeared relaxed, easy…but maybe she'd just been exhausted?

When he'd invited her for lunch it had been clear she'd got the wrong message, and that had confused him again. She'd turned him down flat. And he might have been a little stung, and countered by being too direct with his clarification.

It wasn't as if the thought of lunch with Autumn hadn't entered his mind. Just not quite in the way she'd interpreted.

He wasn't sure what to do next to put any of this right.

Autumn was gorgeous. She was also from another country and would go right back there when her surgeries were complete.

He had a little girl to think of. No matter how attracted he might be to any woman, Sofia had to come first. Always.

The truth was he would take Autumn out in a heartbeat. It had been a long time since he'd had this kind of a reaction to a woman. Not even with his wife.

He had always played his cards close to his chest. His relationship with Anna had been rocky. They'd already decided to go their separate ways when Anna had announced she was pregnant. They'd reached an agreement to give their marriage another chance, and he'd marvelled as his wife's body had bloomed in pregnancy. He'd wondered if having a child would make Anna feel more settled. But it had become clear shortly after Sofia was born that she didn't.

It hadn't been any great surprise to Giovanni. His heart had already told him that was how she felt. Oh, Anna had loved their child. She'd doted on Sofia. But she'd struggled with being a mother. She'd wanted to return to work before her maternity leave was over. Not that Giovanni had minded.

He'd never told anyone they'd already had discussions about formally separating and sharing access to Sofia. Anna had worked in the same hospital and Giovanni would never have spoken ill of his wife. Even though Sofia was too young to remember her, Giovanni had always made sure that every memory he repeated of Anna was good. Sofia even had a large photo on her chest of drawers, of Anna, beaming with happiness, holding baby Sofia in her arms.

He liked that photograph. It held happy memories. And those were the ones he preferred to keep, rather than memories of the exasperation that Anna had clearly felt when they'd fought. She'd told him she felt like a trapped bird. And he, in turn, had told her to spread her wings and fly. Their marriage had never been supposed to be a trap—for either of them—and if Anna hadn't been killed in the accident he was sure they would have managed to part in a fairly amicable way.

Instead he'd been left widowed, a single dad shrouded with doubts. Accidents were rife in Rome. But part of him had always wondered if Anna had been gripped by a moment of madness and thought of another escape.

It was ridiculous. And he knew it. She'd never expressed any suicidal tendencies. But late at night, when sleep was far from him, Giovanni's mind sometimes wandered into scary places. It might just be that he was avoiding the huge amount of guilt he felt about their parting words and their harsh argument. That had stayed with him—the fact that the last words between them had been in anger.

So, having a strong attraction to someone new was more than a little unexpected. Of course, he'd flirted, and occasionally dated over the last year or so. But no one had made his heart skip a few beats. Not even one. Until now.

He sighed and headed down to the hospital canteen, grabbing some food before joining a table with three other staff members. He could see the gleam in their eyes—all of them filled with hope that they would join one of the teams. They were hungry for it, and that made him glad. Hunger was what he looked for. Only the best would be allowed on his team. But first and foremost they had to really, really *want* it.

He didn't mind the reasons. To be part of precision surgery, for research, for the prestige of being part of a separation, or simply pure and utter passion for the project. Just as long as they had that passion.

He gave an easy smile and joined in their chat, only to be instantly distracted by the sight of Autumn walking through the doors. Her dark hair was slightly damp and piled above her head, and she was wearing a fresh pair of burgundy scrubs. She grabbed a sandwich and headed towards their table.

He could see the tiniest flash of hesitation in her face, and it made him sad, but Autumn sat down with ease, joining in the conversation at the table in a mixture of English and stumbling Italian. Her shoulders were tense and it took a little time for them to ease.

He kept on eating, nodding slowly and joining in. He was determined not to allow any of the others to pick up on any discord between them. Even he wasn't entirely sure if it was there or not. Maybe it was all just in his head and he was reading more into things than he should? Maybe parts of his brain were sparking back to life after slumbering for too long? But the truth was the other three were too busy trying to impress to pick up anything.

A few other people joined the table, one bringing coffee for both Autumn and Giovanni in a shameless ploy. Another brought a tray of donuts for the whole table. This doctor winked at the others and shrugged his shoulders at his colleague with the coffee. 'Hey, I didn't want to make it too obvious I'm trying to buy affection here. So I just bought for everyone.'

The rest of the people at the table laughed. All of them knew there was only one thing on their minds. The surgeries.

Giovanni watched Autumn. She was deep in conversation with the fellow surgeon sitting next to her. It was interesting to observe—particularly as he was a surgeon he'd planned to include in his own team, and Autumn had teased him about poaching.

As their conversation continued Giovanni shifted in his chair, wondering if it would be childish to interrupt. But before the thought could progress any further Autumn turned and gave him a stare that was a cross between haughty and challenging. His coffee slid down his throat the wrong way and he half coughed, half choked.

She pushed back her shoulders, lifted her eyebrows, and turned with her biggest grin back to the other surgeon.

Giovanni felt a wave of relief. Maybe he had overthought things. She certainly seemed to be relaxed enough now. That had seemed like a challenge. As if she were telling him, *I'm stealing your surgeon.*

He looked around the table and started talking. 'You'll all be well aware that Autumn and I still have to make selections for Team Hope and Team Grace. What you might not know is that this morning Autumn and I did our first practice surgery. There will be others—many others—and you will all have the chance to be involved. Our babies are at twenty-six weeks right now. We will need to have our teams in place, if possible, within the next few weeks. Whilst we hope our babies will remain in utero for as long as possible, we also know that we could be called at any moment.'

Everyone had stopped talking when Giovanni started, but the silence that fell around the table now was heavy. It wasn't that his potential team didn't already know how serious this was, but he could see a few of them swallowing with difficulty.

The only person who didn't look fazed at all was Autumn. Her shoulders remained straight and her gaze steady. A little buzz shot through

him. She would be ready at a moment's notice.
Just as he would. That instilled him with confidence. For him and for the babies.

'My door is open for anyone who wants to talk
to me about being on my team,' he said, knowing Autumn would see the glint in his eye.

'As is mine,' she added promptly.

She stood up and moved alongside him. She
was making sure that everyone knew they were
equals.

And they were.

Things seemed more relaxed now. What had
happened earlier today must surely have been
a blip.

He was still thinking when she turned to him.
'I have some work to do. I'll catch you later.'

Before he had a chance to reply, Autumn
strode away across the canteen. He could see
several staff members watching her leave, and
he could almost write a list of who might approach her.

He tried not to smile. Healthy competition
among staff was good. Everyone would be working at their optimum level to ensure a place on
a team.

And that was entirely what he wanted—all
staff at their absolute best to ensure the best possible outcomes for these babies.

CHAPTER FIVE

Autumn couldn't pretend she didn't feel a bit off. Whilst she'd had relationships with colleagues in the past, they'd never been with men she might potentially look at across the operating table.

The host of emotions that had swept over her while practising with Giovanni were simmering beneath her surface. It didn't matter how much she tried to ignore things, the air between them definitely sizzled.

Her brain told her it was too soon. She'd only just had a text to say that all her clothes had been packed up and delivered to her flat.

She pulled at her bright pink shirt. She hadn't asked for her clothes to be delivered to Italy. It would have been ridiculous and costly, and she'd rapidly realised the clothes she'd normally wear in the UK were just too warm for the current weather in Rome.

Her only choice was an immediate new wardrobe.

Via del Corso was one of the main streets in the historical centre of Rome, and several of the female staff at the hospital had pointed her in this direction to get some elegant dresses and suits for work.

Autumn couldn't believe quite how long and straight this street was, compared to the surrounding area that was littered with alleys and a variety of small *piazze*. What was also interesting was how narrow the street was by modern standards. It was busy, with only two lanes of traffic, and the pavements were packed with shoppers.

The buildings were a variety of colours— oranges, yellows, creams and a few red—with designer shop signs flickering in the light wind. The temperature was high today, and Autumn knew that as soon as she bought some new clothes, she would wear them straight from the boutique.

As she jostled with the crowds and listened to the chatter around her, she realised that there were just as many tourists as there were locals.

She strolled into the first designer boutique, pulled in by the elegant dresses displayed in the window. As she touched the first, the fabric light against her fingers, she knew it was perfect—

just what she was looking for. The only trouble was the sharp intake of breath behind her.

She turned around. A woman in a beige suit was looking down her nose at her, speaking in rapid Italian. Autumn caught a few words and made a stammering attempt to reply in Italian. The woman wrinkled her nose, and Autumn felt embarrassed. She was surprised. These Italian boutiques must be filled with tourists on a regular basis.

She tried a few words in English. 'Excuse me, I'm looking for some dresses…' She lifted her hand again, wanting to check the size label on the dress, but the saleswoman stepped in front of her.

Autumn was immediately self-conscious, looking down at her clothes. She had on black trousers and a pink shirt. They were certainly a few years old, but perfectly serviceable. She had the most uncomfortable feeling that the woman didn't think she was good enough to shop in this boutique.

Maybe she was misunderstanding? Maybe it was just a language barrier—and that flooded her with guilt. She was trying her best, but after less than two weeks she certainly hadn't mastered the language by any means.

The woman spoke to her again, rapidly and

not entirely pleasantly. Autumn didn't need to understand the words to understand the tone.

She took a final glance at the emerald-green dress that would have been perfect, before giving a polite nod of her head and walking out of the door.

Her phone started ringing instantly, and she pulled it from her bag and answered it without even glancing to see who was calling.

'Hi.' Her voice was abrupt as frustration swept through her.

'Autumn? What's wrong?'

Giovanni's voice was like an instant balm. She wasn't thinking about earlier that week. Or about how she'd spent the last few nights barely sleeping, whilst he'd danced around in her thoughts.

'I've come shopping—' she sighed '—and I'm having some trouble.'

'What kind of trouble?' he sounded instantly concerned.

Now she felt a bit pathetic. 'I think it's just a language thing…'

'Where are you shopping?'

'Via del Corso. I wanted some lighter clothes for work. You know…smart, but something I can actually breathe in.'

He gave a soft laugh. 'Are you at one of the designer stores?'

She nodded, then realised he couldn't see her. 'Yes.'

'Give me a name?'

She turned and looked back at the pale-green-fronted store she'd just left and read the name out to Giovanni.

He gave a loud sigh. 'I told you to let me know when you needed to shop.'

'Don't be ridiculous. I don't expect you to come shopping with me.'

'Order a coffee at one of the nearby stands. I'll be there in ten minutes and I will take you to some places where they'll treat you the way they should.'

She didn't have a chance to say no before he hung up. She looked up at the door sign again. It was as if he actually knew something about the place.

She moved over to a coffee stand with a few tables and ordered coffee for both of them, sitting for a bit and watching the world go by. The heart of Rome was extraordinary. Partly filled with tourists, but also some of the most stylish people she'd ever seen.

A woman in a pale pink trouser suit with a bright silk scarf knotted at her throat strolled past as if she were wearing the most casual clothes in the world. Another woman moved along on the other side of the slim street, designer sunglasses on her face and wearing an elegant pure white dress that rippled around her model-slim frame. The crowd parted like the Red Sea around her, and Autumn held in a giggle.

She jumped as Giovanni sat down in the chair opposite her.

'There you are.' He beamed as if they were best friends.

'You didn't need to come,' Autumn said hastily. 'I'm sure I could have managed.'

He pointed down the street to the store she'd been in. 'Not in there. They're notorious. I'll show you where to shop.' His eyes ran down her body. 'There's some great places around here. Do you have a price range?'

Some might be offended by a question like that, but Autumn wasn't at all. 'As long as we're not in the thousands, I'll be fine.'

He gave a nod, and she saw that he followed her gaze as she watched another woman in a dark green knee-length jersey dress stop to buy coffee from a nearby stand. 'I'd like that kind of thing,' she said. 'Smart enough for work, but still comfortable.'

'Dresses. No problem. Anything else?'

She thought for a moment. Whilst she might be a little embarrassed by Giovanni helping her shop, she might as well take advantage of the moment. 'Some tunic tops, a pair of shorts and some sandals...'

Giovanni laughed. 'You do realise I'll be in big trouble tonight, don't you?'

Autumn's brow furrowed. 'Why?'

'Sofia. She'll be annoyed that she's missed out on a shopping trip.'

'She likes shopping?' Autumn was surprised. Sofia hadn't struck as her a girl who would enjoy shopping trips.

'Are you kidding? My girl can shop like a pro. She *loves* shopping. When I tell her about this I'll be in so much trouble.' Giovanni let out a laugh as he shook his head. 'In fact, so will you.'

Something burned deep down inside her. He spoke about his daughter with so much pride— as he should. She could picture Sofia's face right now. 'I'm not too sure I want to get into an argument with your daughter,' she said with a smile as she stood up and put her bag strap over her head. 'I fear I might lose.'

He grinned as he stood up too. 'Oh, you definitely will. Come on, let's find some stores that are more fun.'

Autumn was amazed by how remarkably easy Giovanni was around the designer stores. He pointed at a few windows, unconcerned when she shook her head. Then they strolled down the street to look in some others.

When Autumn found a store with a large array of dresses in the window display that caught her eye, she was amazed when Giovanni greeted the sales assistant by name. Fifteen minutes later Autumn had found three dresses that she loved.

'The pink is great on you,' said the assistant, Marie, in easy English. 'And the floral print is so light. It will suit you in the hospital.'

'How did you know I worked in a hospital?' asked Autumn as she pulled the third dress, a comfortable green jersey, over her head.

Marie shrugged behind her. 'Giovanni told me you're work colleagues.'

'You're…friends?' Autumn asked as a button from the dress tangled in her hair.

Marie was a petite blonde, very attractive and equally nice. Was Autumn missing something here? And why did she feel a bit odd about that?

Marie leaned forward to unravel Autumn's hair. 'Yes, we're old friends. I know his sisters and I used to know his wife.' She shot Autumn a sorrowful smile.

'Thanks,' said Autumn as she shook out her freed hair.

She was glad of the distraction. Her stomach had clenched uncomfortably, but she was glad Marie hadn't tiptoed around about her. The staff at the hospital sometimes mentioned Anna. Almost in reverent tones. It was a little disconcerting at times, hearing how wonderful and beautiful Giovanni's dead wife had been.

Autumn gave Marie a little nod. 'Yes, Giovanni has told me about his wife. Obviously I'm new to the hospital, and didn't know her, but I've met Sofia. She's a delight.'

Marie's smile broadened. 'Well, if you've met Sofia, you know who the boss is.' She glanced through the curtain towards the front of the store, where Giovanni was patiently waiting. 'It's such a shame he's on his own now.' She gave Autumn a sideways smile. 'We all keep hoping he might meet someone new.'

Heat rushed into Autumn's cheeks. Oh, no, it was like being a teenager back at school. In a few moments she'd gone from wondering if she might be a little jealous to wondering if Marie was trying to set her up. From one extreme to the other. And Marie's steady blue eyes were clearly sizing her up.

Marie tipped her head to one side. 'That's three dresses now. Do you need anything else?'

'S-sandals,' stuttered Autumn. Anything to distract the woman. 'And a few casual tops— maybe some capri pants.'

She didn't want to think about what all this might do to her credit card. It wasn't as if she couldn't afford to buy herself nice things—it was just she hadn't seen a single price tag on any of the items of clothing she'd tried so far. History told her that was never good a sign. It was just as well she loved everything that she'd tried.

Marie appeared again, as if by magic, with a pair of white capri pants and a short-sleeved fitted blouse that was white with pink flowers. She also had with her a second pair of capri pants, in navy, alongside a bright orange loose tunic top with a tie at one side, and a pair of flat cushioned sandals with some sparkle along the straps.

Autumn opened her mouth to talk, but promptly closed it again, taking the clutch of clothes hangers and closing the curtain on the dressing room.

Five minutes later she was glad she hadn't voiced any concerns. Marie's eye was good. She'd picked colours and styles that both suited and complemented Autumn's colouring. What was more, the clothes were actually comfortable. Almost unheard of unless it was a pair of pyjamas.

She kept on the sandals and the navy blue capris and orange top, and handed over the rest for bagging.

'Thank you,' she said to Marie appreciatively. 'You've made this so painless. I've got exactly what I need. How much do I owe you?'

Marie grinned and nodded over to Giovanni,

who was sipping coffee in the corner of the store. 'Not a thing. Your bill has been covered.'

Autumn's credit card was already in her hand. 'What?'

Marie shrugged. 'Whether it's a friend or a sister, he always does this.'

There was something in the way she was looking at Autumn, with a hint of curiosity and humour.

Autumn spun around to Giovanni. 'You can't pay for my clothes! It's nice, but it's far too generous.' She was trying not to sound defensive and annoyed. Was this because he'd asked her what her price range was? Did he think she couldn't afford the clothes?

She heard the rustle of tissue paper behind her as Marie wrapped the dresses and other items, putting them in large bags. It was clear she was staying out of this fight.

Giovanni put down his coffee cup and stood up. He was wearing light trousers and a pale blue shirt, and with that darn dark stubble and the sunglasses on his head he might easily pass for some Italian model.

He gave her a nonchalant shrug. 'I like to keep the women in my life happy. You needed clothes.' He swept his arm out. 'We got you clothes.'

One of the women in his life. That was how

he'd just referred to her. She was momentarily stunned. She couldn't even turn her head, because she was pretty sure that Marie's gaze would be searing into her.

Autumn took a deep breath and moved right in front of him. 'But, Giovanni, you can't pay for my clothes. It's not…' She struggled to find the right word.

'Not what?' He threw up his hands. 'Anyway, I might ask you for a little favour in return.'

Her skin prickled. 'What kind of favour?'

Giovanni threw back his head and laughed. 'You should see your face right now! Don't be silly. This will be fun.' He gave a thoughtful nod of his head. 'Better grab those bags.'

Autumn smiled quickly as she thanked Marie again, and left the shop clutching the large packages. Giovanni started to stroll back in the direction they'd started from. She was still a little uncomfortable. When was the last time a man had bought her clothes? She struggled to remember. It had obviously been a *long* time ago.

He named a popular movie from the nineteen-nineties. 'Ever seen it?'

She looked at him in confusion. 'Of course.'

His smile widened. 'Do you remember that scene where the women in a designer store are mean to the heroine and she returns later with lots of bags?'

Autumn looked down. She was carrying bags from the store that had been nice to her. She glanced up and saw the pale green store in the distance and started to laugh. 'Really? You want to do that?' She wrinkled her nose. 'Do people really do that kind of thing?'

The movie was playing in her head now, and she was seeing the similarities that she hadn't even considered. It might be fun…but it was also out of the ordinary.

She looked at Giovanni curiously. 'Is there something you're not telling me?'

If she hadn't been watching closely she might not have noticed the slight falter in his next footstep. He gave the briefest of nods. 'Maybe. Let's just say I have history with someone who works in that store. I can't believe they're still in business. They treat almost everyone the way they treated you today.'

Autumn's footsteps slowed. 'But why? Why not be like Marie? Why not be nice to people? I've never worked in retail, but surely that makes for better sales?'

Giovanni shook his head. 'I haven't worked in retail either, but courtesy goes a long way—no matter what field you work in.' He looked along the street. They were rapidly approaching the other store. 'Now, why not just have a little fun?'

Temptation was running through her veins. It

felt like something a sixteen-year-old would do. But she couldn't pretend it wasn't a little amusing. Sad thing was, she probably would have bought a number of things in the other store if they'd been a little more friendly. Could she really pull this off?

He slowed as they approached the main door. Her bags were emblazoned with the name of the store Marie worked at. She guessed it must be a rival. Before she could overthink things, Autumn strode into the store. For a few seconds her wave of confidence evaporated, and then she lifted her head and started to stroll around, looking at the items on the rack.

Three saleswomen were standing gossiping at the back. As soon as they saw the amount of designer bags she was carrying, two of them were over in a few seconds. One of them was very familiar.

'Welcome, how can we help you?'

'Would you like some coffee? Some wine, perhaps?'

Autumn gave them a pleasant smile, but didn't attempt to speak. Didn't they even recognise her—remember that she'd been in their store only a few hours before? She started walking along the rails, looking at the clothes.

'What about this? It's one of our finest?'

One of the women had snatched a white jacket

from the rail. It was as about as far removed from any item Autumn would ever wear as it was possible to be.

Autumn gave a brief shake of her head and kept moving.

The other woman moved seamlessly ahead of her, picking out a beige formal dress. 'Something in this shade?' Before Autumn had a chance to object it was pressed against her. 'This colour is perfect for you,' the woman cooed.

Autumn held up her bags and smiled. 'No, thank you. You weren't so helpful when I came in last time, so I shopped elsewhere.' She moved closer to the door and looked over her shoulder. 'Such a shame… You have lovely clothes, and I probably would have bought quite a lot.'

That was enough. That was more than enough.

She could remember the scene from the film exactly in her head, but she wasn't about to make any comments about commission.

Instead she finished with a steady gaze. 'Being nice is so important. We can have no idea of what kind of day another person has had, and I always try to remember that.'

She walked out through the door where Giovanni was waiting. 'You were nice to them,' he said in a surprised tone. 'You might even have taught them a lesson.'

'I doubt it,' she said, just as she heard a sharp voice behind her.

'Giovanni?'

She turned around in time to see one of the saleswomen, with an expression on her face that was a mixture of pinched and haughty. Her words came out in rapid Italian.

Giovanni crossed his arms across his chest. His voice was low, deep, and from its tone Autumn could tell he had no intention of getting into a conversation with this woman.

The woman started throwing her arms about, her voice getting more staccato. Surely he hadn't said anything that bad? There hadn't been time.

Giovanni's voice remained low and steady. And as the woman kept ranting, he slid his arm into Autumn's and dropped into English. 'I think it's time for a change of scenery and I know just the place.'

He shot the woman a disdainful glance and started walking. They'd only gone a few steps when another woman approached him.

Autumn's head was spinning. What on earth was going on—all she'd wanted was a few dresses!

But this woman was entirely different. She was small, dressed in jeans and light shirt, with a broad smile across her face. Before Autumn had a chance to catch her breath the woman had flung her arms around Giovanni and stuck a kiss on his cheek. She was talking nineteen to the dozen, but clearly very pleased to see him.

Autumn was aware of the curious glance she got from her.

'*Tua moglie?*' the woman asked.

There was an awkward pause, then Giovanni shook his head and replied, '*Un college chirurgo.*'

'Ah!' The woman threw up her hands, grabbed Autumn around the neck and kissed both her cheeks.

Autumn's hands were still full of the shopping bags and she was frozen in bewilderment.

The woman then shook Giovanni's hand again, before hugging him for a second time and walking down the road with a final wave.

Autumn was shaking her head. 'Tell me what just happened!' she said, trying not to laugh out loud.

He put his arm around her back and they started walking again. 'That was the mother of a former patient. I saved her son and she's never forgotten.'

Autumn juggled her bags into one hand. 'And the woman from the store?'

His eyebrows were raised and there was a hint of mischief in his eyes. 'Oh, it's safe to say she hates me, but I never lose a moment's thought over it. It's personal.'

'Not now,' said Autumn quickly. 'You made me complicit, so you'd better tell me why.'

He nodded. 'Fair enough. I found out a few years ago that she was cheating customers— charging even more inflated prices than the designer brand had set for their clothes. One of Anna's friends suffered badly from postnatal depression. One of her ways of coping was buying designer clothes frequently and putting them at the back of the cupboard where they wouldn't be found. The family ended up in a large amount of debt.'

He'd mentioned his wife easily, and Autumn shifted a little on her feet. There was always chatter in the hospital. People mentioning how beautiful Anna had been, or what a great doctor she'd been to work with. But things seemed different when it was Giovanni talking about his ex-wife. She didn't like the way it made her feel. Why was that?

'What did you do?' she asked.

He sighed. 'When she asked Anna for help, we discovered the unworn clothes. They still had their tags and the original receipts in the bags. It didn't take long for us to notice that the prices of the items didn't match the prices on the handwritten receipts.'

Autumn's eyes widened. 'That woman did that?'

Giovanni nodded as they walked. 'Celeste— yes. When I confronted her about clearly taking advantage of a vulnerable individual she was furious. But we had all the evidence. The store gave her the choice of paying back the difference to Anna's friend or facing criminal charges.'

'And did she pay the money back?'

Giovanni nodded. 'She did—and then the store sacked her.'

Autumn's footsteps faltered. She squinted her head back. 'So she hasn't always worked in the store I was just in?'

He shook his head. 'No, she's only worked there for the last year, but I heard she was up to her old tricks again.'

Autumn frowned. 'Darn it. Now I want to go back and make more of a scene.'

He rested his other hand on her arm and looked at her thoughtfully. 'Actually, I shouldn't have encouraged you. You were much nicer than I thought you might be. I wish I could say that might have taught her a lesson, but I seriously doubt it.'

They reached a taxi stand and he opened the door of the vehicle at the front. 'After you.'

The taxi driver rushed around and opened the boot, taking Autumn's many bags from her as she climbed in.

It was nice to get out of the heat for a bit

and she settled back in the seat. 'Where are we going?' she asked.

Giovanni slid in beside her. 'How much of the city have you seen? Have you had time to do anything?'

She shook her head.

'So, it might be too hot to go tramping around the sights, but we can have a casual drink with your favourite place in view. Take your pick.'

She pressed her lips together, thinking hard. 'Either the Vatican or the Colosseum. But I'm not sure what the surrounding areas are like.'

He gave her an approving nod. 'Go with your heart. I'll find us somewhere good. I've lived here all my life.'

She closed her eyes for a second then gave a smile. 'The Colosseum, then.'

Giovanni gave some instructions to the driver, and half an hour later led her up some steps to a private rooftop bar, a few streets away from the Colosseum.

She sat down on a plush cream seat, with a large parasol shading them from the hot sun. There was only one other couple on the rooftop and the view of the Colosseum and surrounding bell towers was spectacular.

'Wow...' she breathed as she sat back and re-laxed.

Giovanni was on the bench seat next to her,

his leg close to hers, and he looked over the half-formed structure and smiled widely. 'It's magnificent, isn't it?'

A waiter appeared and handed them both menus, but Autumn's eyes were still on the Colosseum. She couldn't take her eyes off the sight.

Giovanni spoke to the waiter in rapid Italian and he disappeared. She wanted to pinch herself as she stole a glance at Giovanni. She'd noticed the looks he'd got on the street from women, who gave him more than a passing stare.

Whilst she'd been looking for clothes that morning she'd tried to push all thoughts of him from her mind, but then, like magic, he'd appeared, and her wardrobe worries had vanished. Now she was in the perfect place. She just wasn't sure if the man sitting next to her thought he was in the perfect place too.

The waiter brought two glasses of chilled white wine and put them on the shaded table. Giovanni watched as Autumn took a sip from her glass and visibly relaxed.

A smile danced across her face as she looked back at the imposing view. 'I can't quite believe I'm here,' she said quietly. She tipped her head to one side and held up one hand. 'This is right in front of me… Built more than two thousand years ago, a place packed with history where more than fifty thousand people would watch gladiators fight.' She closed her eyes. 'I can almost hear the roar if I try and concentrate.'

He loved that. He loved it that he'd shown her a tiny part of Rome and she was instantly trying to soak it up. He was also feeling a little guilty about what he'd asked her to do earlier.

He'd put most of his life with Anna behind him. But Celeste's manipulation of Anna's friend still made his blood boil.

When he'd heard Autumn's voice on the phone, he had instantly recognised the uncertainty and hurt in her tone. It had struck harder than he could ever have expected. Why? Did he feel protective of his fellow surgeon because he felt responsible for bringing her here and wanted to ensure she stayed for the surgery? That was the easiest explanation. But it didn't quite ring true.

As soon as Autumn had explained where she was, he had known exactly how she was being treated. Giovanni always tried to be logical. First solve the outstanding issue, then go back and deal with the original problem. That was what he always tried to do. But Autumn had handled things better than he had. Every time he found out more about her, it sparked something inside him.

'Bring many people up here?'

Her voice floated through his thoughts. He turned to her with a smile. 'Not many. But the view speaks for itself.'

She held out one hand. 'So does the shade, and…' she raised her glass '…the wine. This is a beautiful place to relax.'

He leaned forward a bit, a teasing edge to his tone. 'What? You don't want to stand in a long queue in the searing heat?'

She shuddered. 'Tell me that I can do a tour at night some time. That would be perfect.'

He could see her imagining it in her head.

'You know…standing inside as the night air cools and the sun is setting behind me. I can just imagine it.'

'Sounds romantic.' The words were out before he had a real chance to consider them.

Her gaze shifted from the building to him. She gave a thoughtful smile. 'Maybe I'm a hopeless romantic and you've just not discovered that yet.'

There was something about sitting under this cool shaded parasol while the world baked around them… From the moment he'd met her there had been an instant attraction—one he'd tried his best not to act on—but the glances, the smiles, the teasing tones and the full body contact were making it very hard for him to continue to fight something he wasn't entirely sure he wanted to fight.

Anna was long since gone, and the memories of their deteriorating relationship had left scars in his brain. Whilst there had been a few passing flings, there had never been anyone who had met Sofia. He'd deliberately never taken that step before. But Autumn had already crossed that bridge. And he wasn't sure how he felt about that.

All he could concentrate on right now was this woman with her soft brown hair and oh-so-green eyes, dressed in blue capri pants and an orange top, with her sunglasses pushed up on top of her head. She was so close he could see some tiny freckles across the bridge of her nose.

'What's the most romantic thing you've ever done?' he asked, his voice low.

She blinked, and he saw something flash across her eyes. The soft cushions on the bench seat seemed to push them closer together. The smile she gave him looked kind of sad.

'I've not really done anything romantic. Just the normal thing—a few nice dinners.' She gave a shrug. 'Nothing big. Nothing spectacular. I guess I've just not really been in that kind of relationship.'

Something pinged hard in his heart. In front of him was a gorgeous, intelligent woman. But she hadn't ever had those moments. Giovanni was struck by that. He could think of any number of romantic moments—silly things, gestures that had struck him at the time as a memory to keep and savour. Some before Anna, some with Anna, and a few after. But Autumn couldn't think of any?

'Didn't a boy ever make you a daisy chain when you were a girl?' he asked.

She looked surprised. 'What? No, never.' Then she frowned. 'Did you make someone a daisy chain?'

They were close. So close he could feel the heat from her skin… He grinned. 'I might have.' Then he pulled a face. 'I might even have made two at the same time.'

She let out a gasp of horror and her hand came down gently on his arm. 'The word I have for you doesn't really translate well from the Scottish,' she said, lifting her eyebrows, 'but in England they would call you a cad.'

'A cad? At five?'

'You were double-dating at *five*?' She shook her head and took a drink. 'I think I'm going to need more wine.'

He liked this. He liked this new, completely relaxed version of them. No hospital. No distractions. Just the chance for him to concentrate on the woman right next to him and finally let her set alight the parts of him that he'd been trying to temper.

As he signalled to the waiter for more wine, she gave him a sideways glance. 'But you have sisters—how on earth did they let you away with that?'

He shifted on the cushions, which meant that his hip and leg were pressing next to hers. He'd turned to face her. There seemed to be little need to stay apart.

'They were actually in competition with each other. Both wanted to set me up with a friend.' His grin widened. 'You have a lot to learn about Italian families. You wouldn't have done the same in Scotland?'

She laughed. 'If anyone had given me a daisy chain between the ages of five and fifteen in Scotland, my brother would have likely beat them with a big stick.'

'Hmm…' Giovanni pretended to be thoughtful for a moment, then asked, 'So your brother… you haven't said much about him. Does he still live in Scotland?'

Autumn laughed again. Her hand was still on Giovanni's arm and she gave it a squeeze. 'The question you want to ask is, where *doesn't* he live?'

Giovanni wrinkled his brow. 'What do you mean?'

She made a flyaway movement with her hand.

Giovanni immediately wanted her to put it back on his arm.

'You might have heard of him. My brother is Ryan Fraser.'

It only took a few seconds for the name to click in his brain. He shifted and looked at her in surprise. 'Your brother is Ryan Fraser the billionaire?' Tiny things started to make sense. 'He has his own jet, doesn't he?'

'Yep. That's how I got here. Ryan has places in Melbourne, London, LA, Washington, Spain and a castle in Scotland.'

Giovanni folded his arms across his chest and couldn't help but grin as he shook his head. 'Wow. Your parents must be delighted.' He gave her a nudge. 'A pair of over-achievers—a billionaire, and a brilliant paediatric liver surgeon.'

Their wine glasses had been topped up and he took a sip. But Autumn tensed. It was as if every cell in her body had just contracted before his very eyes. 'They probably would have been.'

His skin prickled. 'Your parents are dead?'

She nodded. But he instantly knew it was more than that.

Her eyes dropped. 'My parents were very... controlling. With both me and Ryan. They were never bad to us. Just very strict. Much more so than any other parents I knew. They were academics. They probably should never have had

children. They hated any element of life that was out of their control. They just wanted to focus on their work. So they tried to control us completely.' She gave a sad sigh. 'I guess it rubbed off a little. Ryan…he's a bit older than me…he managed to get out before I did.'

'You felt as if you had to "get out"?' asked Giovanni.

Her words and general demeanour were alarming. She'd gone from relaxed and composed to almost turning in on herself.

She gave a nervous laugh and shook herself. 'I'm being too dramatic. We just had a kind of odd experience growing up, with parents who made everything rules and demands.' Autumn paused for a moment and licked her lips. 'I guess it was my parents who made me think about childhood psychological trauma for separated conjoined twins.'

He was trying hard to follow the conversation here. She was saying that her parents hadn't been abusive, but Giovanni was wise enough to know that trauma for children came in many different forms. Part of him wanted to change the subject and get back to where they'd been before. But he wouldn't do that. Not when she was opening up to him.

'How so?'

She sipped her wine again. 'I guess that some

of their controlling behaviour rubbed off on me. I didn't actually realise that for a long time—probably only when one of the girls I shared a flat with at medical school had a chat with me about my rules, my lists, and my own controlling behaviour.'

He nodded. 'But you're a surgeon. All of us have an element of control. We have to. When things happen in Theatre, control can be the most important element.' He met her gaze. 'It can save lives.'

She nodded and gave him a grateful smile. 'I know. I get that.'

'And your brother? Does he feel the same as you?'

She shook her head and her mouth curved upwards into a smile, her shoulders relaxing again. 'Oh, Ryan is entirely normal. Not like me at all. My parents' attitude gave him the remarkable determination to succeed at everything he does, but to do it in a completely different way.'

'That seems to have worked out well for him then,' Giovanni remarked. He gave her a sideways grin. 'Do you think he'd still hit me with a stick if I gave you a daisy chain?'

He was trying to read her. He was clocking up all the things she'd said. All the little reveals. But he didn't want to push too far. She'd already told him more than he'd expected her to. Autumn struck him as a bit like himself. She let the world see what she wanted it to see. Other parts of herself she kept locked inside.

After those few moments of tension she now seemed relaxed and comfortable around him, and happy to be close. He could feel the air sparking between them. But maybe it was just the surroundings and atmosphere. He'd hate to misread the situation.

She turned her head towards his, their noses only inches apart. 'Ryan has learned over the years to respect my choices.' She raised her eyebrows. 'Not that he always likes them—and it doesn't take him long to tell me when that happens.'

'What do you do when he does?'

His voice was barely a whisper. He could smell her shampoo, her perfume, her skin. They were *that* close. A tiny little flake of her mascara had smudged right in the corner of one eye. His fingers itched to reach out and touch it.

She moved again, a soft smile on her lips, her nose brushing against his. 'I tell him again,' she whispered, 'to respect my choices.'

Their lips brushed together, and without even looking Giovanni deposited his wine glass back on the table, freeing up one hand to cup her cheek and letting the other reach around her waist.

Her body shifted towards his and her breasts pressed against his chest. This was no crazy X-rated kiss. This was slow. Deliberate. Meaningful.

He doubted the other people on the rooftop would even notice. But Giovanni noticed. He noticed every second of it. The taste of her, the feel of her… The warm skin under his fingers as her top moved a little. The way her hair slid through his hand as he moved it from her soft cheek to the back of her head.

She didn't seem to mind the way his beard must be brushing against her cheek. In fact, her hand came around and she raked her nails through the short stubble. But after the longest moment she pulled back and pressed her forehead against his. 'Wow…' she breathed.

'Wow,' he agreed, staying exactly where he was.

They remained that way for the next few minutes, and then he felt a cold surface next to his arm. He gave the smallest flinch and looked down.

'Sorry…' Her laugh sounded nervous. Her wine glass had remained in her other hand.

Their heads parted and she sagged back against the cushions. The glass was at her lips a moment later and she took a drink, then let out a long slow breath.

Giovanni lifted his own glass, allowing the cool liquid to slide down his throat. What he really needed right now was an ice bucket over his head. Every sense in his body was currently on fire. The heat around them was nothing to the heat between them.

She still looked a little stunned.

'So…' he said gently.

Autumn licked her lips. 'So,' she said carefully, 'I usually don't mix business with pleasure.'

It was like a nail to the heart.

'You've never dated anyone you've worked with?' he asked.

She shook her head. 'Yes and no.' She glanced around, looking for the waiter. 'Do you think we could order some food? This wine is making me light-headed.'

He might have been offended. But she had a gleam in her eye. As if she knew how that had sounded.

He gestured to the waiter and rattled off the names of a variety of small dishes that he knew would arrive quickly, along with a bottle of sparkling water.

Autumn paused until the waiter had left and then continued. 'What I mean is, although I've dated colleagues, they've never actually been on my team—in my speciality.'

His hand reached up and he ran one finger down her soft cheek, finishing in her hair and winding a finger around one of her locks. 'But I'm not in your team,' he said hoarsely.

She took another deep breath and smiled again, her own hand coming up and her fingertips running along his jawline. 'No,' she breathed, 'you're not.'

And before he had time to say anything else her lips connected with his again.

She honestly felt dizzy. Her brain was firing conflicting messages at her.

He's your workmate.

He's the sexiest man you've ever met.

Go with your gut.

He has a child.

She was acting on instinct and not listening to the part of her brain that was screaming *Proceed with caution.* Waiting… She felt as if she had been waiting for this moment all her life. To have a guy who took her breath away sitting next to her, to have a perfect setting, to be in the perfect moment, and for said guy to be looking at her as if she was the most desirable person on the planet.

She'd just ticked every box.

Moments like this didn't happen often. His words had struck a chord with her and she'd opened up about a number of things she never normally would have. She wasn't quite sure where those words had come from. In normal circumstances she would never have revealed those things. But Giovanni had made it easy. There had been no pressing, no judgement. Those words would always have been awkward, but they hadn't felt uncomfortable.

There was just something about this man that made her feel different. Different from the way she'd felt in every other experience she'd had before.

From their earlier conversation, it seemed Giovanni had had his life littered with moments like this, but Autumn couldn't remember a single one.

It must be the perfect time to start creating them.

She wasn't going to wait another second.

This wasn't a jump-on-each-other moment.

This was the perfect kiss, in the perfect place, with the perfect person.

She let out a little groan at the feel of his delicate touch on her skin. The taste of his lips against hers. The scent of his cologne on his skin. Her senses were on fire.

She reluctantly pulled her lips from his just as the waiter put plates of delicious-looking food down on their table, followed by some glasses and a bottle of water.

The sun was starting to dip in the sky, creating reds, oranges and purples. A few people came out onto the rooftop to appreciate the spectacular colours now framing the Colosseum.

Giovanni's arm moved around her shoulders as they leaned forward to grab cutlery.

'What do you think?' he whispered softly, glancing at the skyline in front of them.

She threaded her fingers through his. 'I like the view whichever way I'm looking,' she answered with a smile. 'And I think we should start the way we mean to continue,' she added, before they kissed again.

seem like a man who was a little sad and sorry. It would be nosey to ask why, and it was certainly none of her business. But Autumn couldn't help her natural curiosity.

She also struggled with the idea of responsibility, which for a specialist surgeon she knew was completely crazy. In her career she regularly had the lives of others literally in her hands.

But in her personal life she'd tended to shy away from responsibility. She'd spent the last few years telling herself it was due to the fact that she was trying to get a work/life balance. But the truth was Autumn knew that was garbage. Maybe she was a little terrified she would end up like her parents. Consumed by work, with no room for any family that came along?

She'd never had that burn, that desire to spend every minute of every day with another human being. Maybe if she'd experienced that, things would be different now. It might help her to take the next step. Learn to take a chance and accept the possibility that there could be hurt along the way and every element of her life might not be under her control.

Her life had been generally comfortable… pleasant. Just like her life with Louis. If at some moment he'd proposed, or mentioned children, she would likely have flown into a wild panic.

Because the truth was that 'look' she'd seen

her friends exchange at their wedding had turned something on in her brain. *That* was what she was supposed to experience. *That* was what love was about. And it completely terrified her.

The thought of being that much in love with another person, giving your whole heart to someone, with no real guarantee it would be taken care of, made her anxiety levels soar. It was such a chance to take—letting go of an element of control and trusting another person with all your emotions.

She knew it started with an immediate heart-quickening, overwhelming rush of attraction.

And that was the sensation she'd experienced with Giovanni Lombardi.

Currently nicknamed in her brain as Mr Sex on Legs.

'Dr Fraser?'

The voice knocked her out of her thoughts. Probably just as well.

'Yes, Daniel?' He was a promising resident.

He gestured with his head. 'I was thinking about the formation of the hepatic artery and if there's a way to split it.'

She leaned forward, instantly interested. A major part of her surgery was based around reconstructing one of the major blood vessels to allow Grace's liver to function. She'd already practised numerous ways—using the vessels already present, or trying to create a new one for Grace.

She moved alongside him and listened to his suggestions. All of them she'd already tried— but Daniel didn't know that, and she was glad he was taking the time to concentrate on thinking out of the box for her surgery. He was just the kind of resident she liked to train and develop.

As she bent down she looked over and Giovanni caught her eye. Neither of them was wearing a mask right now, in the clinical training room. There was a half-smile on his face. He raised one eyebrow and shook his head. *He's mine,* he mouthed.

No way, she mouthed back.

This had been their battle for the last few days. Both of them were picking their teams. It was, at times, like a stand-off, when they wanted a particular candidate. Autumn already had eleven on her team. A fellow surgeon, a trainee, an anaesthetist, five theatre nurses and three neonatal staff for the post-operative care of Grace.

But there were many slots on her team still to be filled. So it didn't help that while she was contemplating all these choices her head was full of snippets of Giovanni. A joke he'd made. A look they'd exchanged. She wasn't quite sure where their relationship was. That said, she wasn't quite sure they even actually *had* a relationship.

After he'd dropped her back at the hotel the other evening, she'd spent the remaining part of the night lying in her comfortable bed with the windows flung wide to the warm night air and sleep completely evading her.

What might have happened if she'd wanted to pursue things? What would he have said if she'd invited him up to her hotel room?

Thoughts like that made her pulse race, and her stomach roll. There was always a chance that Giovanni might have refused. And, to be truthful, she was glad she hadn't found out the answer to that potential scenario. Everything was still in her head as the perfect moment, and that was how she wanted it to stay.

But working alongside him every day was making her crazy.

Giovanni clapped his hands loudly, attracting the attention of all in the room. 'Ricardo, Erin, David—we all have a surgery in thirty minutes. It's time to prepare.' He waved his arms and gave the people in the room a broad grin, his eyes meeting hers. 'As for the rest of you—feel free to continue with your practice.'

Was there a secret message there? She didn't think so. But she couldn't pretend she didn't feel a little pull of something as Giovanni left the room.

There was an air about him…a magnetism

that affected every cell in her body. She caught glances from some of the staff, and shouted some more instructions to them, walking slowly around the room and advising wherever she could. Trying to keep her mind on anything but Giovanni Lombardi.

When her pager sounded, her heart missed a dozen beats.

She wasn't on the regular staff here. She hadn't left messages anywhere in the hospital, and nor was she waiting for any tests results. Which meant her pager would only sound if there was an issue with Hope or Grace.

The number on the screen was unrecognisable. She moved to a phone outside the training room and dialled quickly.

The voice was initially Italian, but quickly switched to English. '*Scusi*, I'm looking for Dr Lombardi. He's not answering his pager.'

'Dr Lombardi is in Theatre right now.' Autumn pulled her watch from the pocket of her scrubs and looked at it. 'He will be there for another few hours. Is there anything I can help you with?'

There was a brief pause. 'Dr Lombardi's sister is in the emergency department with his daughter, Sofia. They're asking for him.'

Her heart lurched. Of course she should go and get him. But Giovanni was performing a complicated follow-up surgery on a six-week-old baby with kidney problems.

Autumn took a deep breath. Instinct told her to assess the situation first. If she needed to get Giovanni, then she would.

'I'll deal with them,' she said into the receiver, before replacing the phone.

The ED was busy. It took her a few minutes to locate the unfamiliar woman with Sofia.

'Autumn!' said Sofia in delight as she walked around the curtain.

The woman with Sofia turned her head sharply. She was tall and slim, with dark brown hair and dark eyes. To put it bluntly, she was stunning, and her gaze was wary.

'Where is Giovanni?' she demanded.

Autumn stuck her hands in the pockets of her white coat. She wasn't normally intimidated, but it was strange to know that this was her first meeting with the sister of the man she'd kissed the week before.

She moved over to them, relieved that Sofia looked healthy. 'Giovanni is currently in surgery with a six-week-old baby,' she said softly, catching sight of a large white cotton patch on the top of Sofia's arm. 'Sofia, have you hurt yourself?'

Sofia nodded, looking almost proud of herself. 'I got in a fight,' she said.

Autumn washed her hands and sat down on

a stool next to Sofia, pulling on some gloves. She kept her voice steady and tried her best not to smile.

'The school phoned me,' said Giovanni's sister, who still hadn't introduced herself. 'Sofia injured her arm on the school fence. I thought it might need stitches.'

Autumn gave a nod. 'Sofia, can I have a look at this?'

Sofia nodded, and Autumn pulled up the edge of the soaked cotton swab. Underneath was an angry, jagged tear. Careful stitching would be required, and there was a possibility of some scarring.

A nurse wheeled in a trolley, as if she'd read her mind. She gave Autumn a curious stare, then glanced at her name badge. 'Ah, the paediatric surgeon. Welcome.'

'How do you know each other?' asked Giovanni's sister sharply, her head flicking between Sofia and Autumn.

'We went to dinner together,' said Sofia merrily, 'With Daddy.'

The hostility in the room seemed to move up a few notches.

'Can you call Giovanni, please?' his sister demanded.

Autumn took a deep breath and decided to start again. She took off her gloves and held out her hand to the woman. 'Hi, I'm Autumn Fraser. I'm a paediatric surgeon working with your brother. I've only been here a few weeks, and the first day I arrived your brother and Sofia took me out to dinner to help familiarise me with the area and, I think, to keep me awake after I'd had a very early start.'

The woman blinked. Then she held out her arm, shaking Autumn's hand. 'Eleonora. I'm Giovanni's sister.' Her other hand stroked Sofia's hair fondly. 'I help him out with Sofia.'

Autumn gave Eleonora a warm smile. 'It's lovely to meet you. I'm sorry it's under these circumstances. But let me assure you...' she nodded to Sofia's arm '... I will take good care of Sofia for you.' She paused, letting Eleonora consider her words. Then, 'The surgery that Giovanni is currently involved in is very delicate, and I'm not sure another surgeon could take his place right now.'

There was a flicker of annoyance on Eleonora's face. Or was it worry? Autumn didn't know her well enough to tell the difference.

She turned to Sofia. 'I'm going to clean up your arm, then put a couple of stitches in. Are you okay with me doing that?'

For the briefest moment Autumn thought she saw a little falter in Sofia's confidence, but then she tilted her chin up towards her.

'Can we have gelato after?'

Autumn was careful in her response. 'If your Aunt Eleonora says it's okay, then I'd be happy to get you a gelato.'

After another few seconds Eleonora gave a sigh. 'Okay, then. But you have to let Giovanni know as soon as his surgery is finished. He likes to be notified of anything about Sofia at once.'

'Of course.'

Autumn spoke to one of the nurses, first asking her to leave a message for Giovanni, and second to get some extra supplies, before washing her hands again. She cleaned the wound and used a numbing spray on the area before injecting a little local anaesthetic prior to doing the stitches.

Sofia only gave the slightest flinch, and it only took a few minutes to line up the ragged skin and place the careful stitches. Once she'd dressed the wound, she did a quick check to ensure Sofia's tetanus shot was up to date.

'How about that gelato?' she said as she snapped off her gloves.

Eleonora glanced at her watch. 'It's too late to return to school. I suppose gelato would be okay.' She picked up Sofia in her arms, turning slightly away from Autumn. 'I'll take you.'

'No,' said Sofia quickly, a stubborn tone in

her voice. 'Autumn said she would take me. She promised.'

Autumn suddenly felt like a pawn in a game of family politics.

'Sofia!' Giovanni rushed through the curtains, his face stricken.

'Papà!' Sofia yelled happily.

Autumn stood to the side as rapid Italian flew between the three family members. She was about to retreat discreetly when she felt a firm hand on her arm.

'Autumn, thank you so much for taking care of Sofia for me.'

'No problem. What about your surgery? I didn't expect you to be out for another few hours.'

He gave her a sorry look. 'Turns out we didn't even get started. There was a problem with the baby's clotting factor. We had to delay. Thank goodness we hadn't anaesthetised.'

Autumn pressed her lips together. From the dark furrows on Giovanni's brow she could see someone would clearly be in major trouble about this.

Eleonora started talking again and gave Autumn a sideways glance. But Giovanni waved one hand and started talking over her. Autumn shifted her feet uncomfortably. Why did she feel as if this was an argument about her?

Giovanni seemed to finish speaking abruptly. He walked over and kissed his sister on both cheeks, talking to her in a low voice. A moment later Eleonora kissed Sofia once more, before disappearing out through the curtains.

'Gelato?' asked Giovanni brightly.

Sofia was already clapping her hands, her injury forgotten.

Autumn hesitated for a second. But she wasn't on the clock here. Unless something happened with the twins, no one would page her. Anyhow, she'd be with Giovanni, and they would page him too.

'Gelato sounds good.'

'Yay!' Sofia was still clapping. She tugged at the edge of Giovanni's scrubs. 'You can't wear this for gelato, Papà.'

'You're right. I can't. We'll head up to the locker room.'

Giovanni kept hold of his girl tightly. Autumn could see the relief in his face. She wasn't sure what his thoughts had been when he'd got the message about Sofia being in the emergency department, but from the way he'd burst through the curtains she assumed his heart had been in his mouth.

What was strange for her was the fact that her heart had been in her mouth too when she'd got the message about Sofia. There had been a distinct moment of panic. Autumn had been a doctor too long, and seen too many sights she couldn't un-see, for her head not to sometimes go to the worst-case scenario.

When she'd seen Sofia sitting awake and alert on the cubicle trolley, she'd breathed a huge sigh of relief. And her relief could only have been a fraction of Giovanni's.

They'd reached the locker rooms and Giovanni reluctantly set Sofia back down on the floor. The little girl automatically slid her hand into Autumn's. 'I'll come with you,' she told her. She wrinkled her nose at the sign on the men's locker room. 'That one is always stinky.'

Autumn burst out laughing. 'Okay, come with me to the non-stinky room while I get changed. Meet you in five, Giovanni,' she said over her shoulder as she pushed open the door.

Her locker held the white capri pants and the white shirt with pink flowers she'd bought with Giovanni the week before, and Autumn set them down on the bench as she pulled out her toiletries.

'This is pretty,' said Sofia as she held up the blouse.

'Thank you,' said Autumn as she took off her scrubs and held out her hand for the shirt. 'I bought it in a shop that your *papà* took me to.'

'Auntie Marie's?'

Autumn blinked. 'Marie is your auntie too?'

Sofia smiled. 'I call her that. Auntie Eleonora and Auntie Bella shop there too.'

Autumn gave herself a final spray of perfume and slicked on some lipstick. 'Okay, ready for gelato?'

She held out her hand to Sofia. It seemed like the natural thing to do, even though she wasn't really used to children this age. But Sofia reacted well, and as they walked out Giovanni was waiting, in a white open-necked shirt and light trousers.

He rubbed his hands. 'Our favourite place?' He smiled at Sofia.

'Yes!' she shouted.

He winked at Autumn. 'Let us take you to the best gelateria in Rome.'

All Giovanni could feel right now was relief. He was glad Sofia had only requested gelato, because he probably would have agreed to anything. When he'd been in Theatre and had got that message, his heart had pounded so much he'd thought he might die.

His staff were intelligent enough not to have passed on the message about his daughter when he was in the middle of surgery, but as soon as his surgery had been cancelled one of the theatre nurses had quickly come in and whispered in his ear.

He'd taken off like a rocket. And he'd never been so glad to see Autumn in a cubicle. It had given him instant reassurance that Sofia was in good hands.

He took a breath for a moment. That was an unusual thought for him. Usually no one was good enough for his daughter. He remembered one night when her temperature had soared, and he'd thought the doctor in the emergency department too inexperienced and had demanded his superior.

He cringed now at how ridiculous that seemed. But thankfully his colleagues had forgiven him and Sofia had been fine.

It was odd, though. Because he frequently took referrals from other hospitals, with parents who demanded 'the best' to assess their child, often not accepting the opinion of their local surgeon who, most times, would make the same recommendation for their child. Being a parent had made Giovanni understand that behaviour, and he looked at Autumn curiously. How did she feel about those kind of referrals?

A taxi dropped them in front of Regallo's and they jumped out. Sofia dashed to her favourite seat at one of the white metal tables.

He pulled out a chair for Autumn and waited

until she was seated. 'What's your favourite fla-
vour?' he asked.

'Raspberry,' answered Autumn, with a broad
smile on her face.

She was wearing the clothes he'd bought for
her last week, and she looked fabulous. He nodded.

'What's yours?' she asked.

'Melon.'

'What?'

He shrugged. 'I can't explain it. It's always
been my favourite since I was a child.' He
nudged his daughter. 'And, Sofia, do you want
to tell Autumn what your favourite is?'

'Chocolate and banana,' his daughter said
without a moment of hesitation. 'With sauce.'

Autumn smiled. 'This gelato sounds like it
might be fun.'

They ordered, and as soon as the gelato arrived Sofia was engrossed.

'Thank you,' said Giovanni.

Autumn looked up, spoon in hand. 'For what?'

'For looking after Sofia today.'

Autumn looked surprised. 'Of course. No
problem at all.' Her mouth gave a tiny pull. 'She
will likely have a tiny scar. But I hope it will
fade with time. I never asked her about the fight
where it happened, though.'

Giovanni gave Autumn a careful look, then

aimed his eyes at his daughter. She caught on immediately.

'Sofia,' said Giovanni carefully. 'Do you want me to tell me why you were fighting at school today?'

Sofia's spoon paused midway to her mouth. She sighed and rested it at the edge of her dish. 'It was Enzo, Papà,' she said. 'He's mean to everyone.'

'Was he mean to you?'

She rolled her eyes. 'He tried to be. I wouldn't take it.' Sofia waved her hand, flicking chocolate sauce everywhere.

Autumn gave a little signal with her finger and Giovanni realised she wanted to take over the questioning. He watched as she leaned down so her head was level with Sofia's.

'So…tell me what he did?'

Sofia turned her full attention to Autumn. 'He stole my friend's *cioccolato*. I shouted at him and he pushed me into the fence.'

Giovanni bristled. And he saw that Autumn was automatically defensive.

'That's how you got hurt?' she asked.

Sofia nodded. 'But so did he.' She picked up her spoon again.

'What does that mean?' Autumn's tone was gentle, but curious.

Sofia grinned. 'I kicked him in the leg. Twice.'

Autumn pressed her lips together and glanced at Giovanni. The temptation to jump in was strong. This was his daughter. It was up to *him* to enforce what was right and what was wrong. But something made him stop.

Autumn put her hand on Sofia's. 'Do you think there might have been any other way to sort this out? One that meant you didn't end up with stitches and Enzo didn't have a sore leg?'

Sofia frowned instantly, her bottom lip pouting, but after a few moments she gave another sigh. 'I could have talked to the teacher...'

Autumn smiled. 'You could have. And that might have saved a visit to the emergency department.' She put her hand on her chest, where her heart was. 'I got a real fright when someone told me you were in the emergency department.' Her eyes met Giovanni's. 'I know your *papà* did too.' She lowered her voice. 'And I bet that Aunt Eleonora was upset about the call from school too.'

Sofia's shoulders slumped a little, as if her initial bravado was finally fading.

'Lots of people worry about you, honey. Everyone wants you to be safe.'

It only took a few moments for Sofia's doleful eyes to meet Giovanni's. He was completely and utterly biased, and he knew it, but his daughter could break his heart with one glance.

'Sorry, Papà,' she said quietly.

He did his best to stay silent for a moment. He was impressed by how Autumn had handled things. Was this a woman's touch with his daughter? He was much too fiery. His first reaction on hearing that a little boy had caused scarring to his daughter had been to want to yell at the world. Rage had raced through him. Then his rational brain had kicked into place within a few seconds, but he was conscious of his initial fierce protectiveness of his little girl—his whole world.

It had been a childhood spat. The kind that the school would handle on a regular basis. This one had just had unfortunate consequences. He was sure if he checked his phone there would be a call from one of the teachers. He would deal with that later.

'I'm glad you're safe,' he said throatily, trying to hide the emotion welling in his voice as he reached over and rubbed the top of her unaffected arm.

'Will you take my stitches out?' Sofia had turned to Autumn again.

This time Autumn looked a little nervous. It was clear she thought Giovanni would want to supervise that action himself, but he shook his head. 'We'll invite Autumn round next week and she can take them out for us at home.' He raised a questioning eyebrow. 'If that's okay with you?'

'Of course,' she agreed quickly, and then she tilted her head slightly and she gave him a quizzical look.

'I'm glad you were there today,' he admitted. 'I think my hands might have been—how do you put it?—all fingers and thumbs if I'd tried to stitch my own daughter.'

Autumn gave him a gracious nod. They both knew that a doctor wasn't really supposed to treat a member of their own family, but they also knew it happened all the time.

'I was glad I was there and able to help.' She touched the top of Sofia's covered arm gently. 'I think you'll have a little pink scar that will fade to white in time. You probably won't even notice it when you're older.'

She gave her a soft smile, and something shifted inside Giovanni. He'd been trying so hard to put their time together at the rooftop bar in a safe place. It had been an exception to his rule of not mixing his personal life with his professional life. When he'd dated colleagues before, it had never been someone in his team or involved in his surgeries. He also didn't introduce potential girlfriends to his daughter.

But it seemed he'd spent the last few weeks

throwing all his rules out of the window. Today was an exception.

That was what he was currently trying to tell himself as he watched Sofia and Autumn together. They talked easily, but he could tell Autumn felt just a little awkward. Maybe she wasn't used to kids Sofia's age, and that was fine, but she was making an effort. And Sofia liked her. In fact, Autumn appeared to be his daughter's favourite topic of conversation.

He could only imagine the phone call later from his sister, Eleonora. He sensed she hadn't quite approved, but Giovanni had spent years doing battle with his feisty sisters, so that was nothing unusual.

Sofia put her hand up to Autumn's ear and whispered something to her conspiratorially, and they both looked at him and laughed.

'What?' he asked indignantly.

Sofia giggled and pointed her finger at his chest. There, on the pale blue shirt, was a stray drip of chocolate sauce. He groaned as he picked up a napkin, knowing it was stained for life.

'How did I get chocolate sauce on my shirt when I didn't even have any?'

Sofia's head bent next to Autumn's and the two of them started laughing again.

Giovanni's throat dried. It hit him in an instant. How much his daughter was missing by not having a mother. It wasn't that he'd never thought about it before—of course he had. But he'd convinced himself that his sisters filled that gap in Sofia's life, and up until this point had considered himself lucky.

He'd always done his best to be everything his daughter needed, but right now the simple moment of seeing the connection between her and Autumn made him feel like a failure.

It was like a punch to the gut.

He'd got this wrong. Sofia was bonding with Autumn—a woman he barely knew. He had no idea what she thought about kids—what she thought about him. He was allowing his daughter to see something that might not exist. This simple act of bringing Autumn with them for ice-cream might become a whole lot more in a five-year-old's head.

He should have known better.

That was his job.

To protect his daughter.

He stood up sharply and both Autumn and Sofia looked up in surprise. 'I'll just pay, then Sofia and I need to head home. I'll drop you back at your hotel, Autumn.'

He couldn't pretend that he didn't see the flash of hurt in her eyes. But he'd think about that later. Right now, he needed to get out of here.

Process what had happened today and work out what on earth was currently going on in his life.

Because one thing was clear.

Giovanni didn't have a clue.

CHAPTER SEVEN

AUTUMN PULLED HER clothes out of the large carved wooden wardrobe. It was the kind of luxury item normally spotted in a country house, but here it was in the middle of her hotel room in Rome.

Four weeks. That was how long she'd been here. And even though she knew Rome had hills, she'd never expected it to be such a rollercoaster.

She'd thrown her windows open this morning and to her delight there had been a tiny smatter of rain. It had actually reminded her of Scotland, even though the noises and smells were completely different here.

Her hand ran across the soft green dress Giovanni had bought for her, and she almost rejected it from that memory alone.

She had no idea what was wrong with him. Maybe he was still upset about Sofia's little accident. But Sofia had appeared none the worse to Autumn. In fact, in two days' time she should be taking out the little girl's stitches.

But Giovanni had been distant with her. It could be anxiety. Gabrielle Bianchi had been feeling unwell yesterday—although there had been nothing wrong that anyone could find. Both of them were on edge in case the babies arrived early. But Lizzy and Leon had spent all day examining their patient, reassuring everyone that there was nothing of immediate concern, and Autumn trusted their judgement.

In fact, she was meeting Lizzy this morning, for their long-awaited coffee.

She shouldn't be nervous, but she was a little. Lizzy had amazing credentials as a neonatal cardiac specialist. The surgery that she and Leon had performed had been essential to the survival of the girls.

Autumn froze. When had she started calling Hope and Grace that? The girls?

She made a grab and pulled the soft green dress over her head. She liked it, it was comfortable and stylish, and whether or not Giovanni had paid for it was irrelevant.

She took another quick glance around the room, looking for her bag. With its giant four-poster bed, thick carpet and curtains, it was one of the most luxurious hotel rooms she'd ever stayed in. The thought of going back to her virtually empty flat didn't fill her with joy. She imagined her boxes, piled high in her sitting room, waiting to be unpacked.

Something twisted inside her. A sense of failure? Or a sense of loneliness?

Ever since she'd arrived in Rome and met Giovanni her head had been in turmoil. Her emotions were all over the place, and it didn't help that everyone in the hospital gave the impression that his dead wife, Anna, had been some kind of saint. How could she live up to that?

Growing up, she'd been used to feeling emotionally isolated. For her it was learned behaviour. Could she be capable of unlearning that?

Her brain kept going back, time and time again, to those romantic moments that everyone else on the planet seemed to have had except her. She never threw caution to the wind. Especially not with her heart. And not for the first time it struck her that she might end up on her own.

As an independent woman, that shouldn't worry her in the least—and on some points it didn't. But on others she wanted to hope that she could share her life with someone. Have a happy-ever-after like in the movies. But would that even be a remote possibility for her? She was starting to think that she might have sabotaged previous relationships by never really letting go. Never letting herself truly love someone and be truly loved in return.

Giovanni's face floated into her head again. That sexy smile, those deep dark eyes… She could swear her heart gave some kind of pang. She had never, ever felt like this about someone before.

That twist inside continued. She'd never wanted to let go. She'd always wanted to keep a piece of herself back. It helped with her feelings of being in control, being in charge.

But was life really all about always being in charge? Or could she trust herself to hand that piece of her heart into someone else's hands?

She shook her head and strolled across the room, grabbing her bag before heading out. She had to stop second-guessing every thought she had. Surgery—that was what she had to focus on right now.

Autumn had actually started to enjoy her commute to the hospital and around Rome. She liked the hustle and bustle of the people—even on the packed public transport. She picked up snatches of conversation. Her Italian was slowly but surely becoming a little better. Her attempts at conversation were still—in a word her brother would use—dodgy, but her understanding was improving every day.

She smiled now, as she heard two women a little younger than she was, discussing the merits of a particular group of men. She watched a young mother juggle a baby on her lap along with a few shopping bags. And she admired a conversation between two teenagers who were clearly at the first stages of flirting.

People were living life all around her, and Autumn was struck with a wave of sadness.

What did she have in life? Sure, she had a brilliant career, some good friends and her own place. She also had her health, and she'd met enough people in this lifetime to know that, for some, that was all they would ever want. So now she felt selfish. But that didn't stop the wave of emptiness that echoed inside her.

She'd never thought like this before. And she knew exactly why.

Giovanni.

There was something about the guy. And not just his electric kisses. The buzz in the air from that first look…

She'd never have dreamed that she'd be interested in a man with a child before. But Sofia was drawing her in. The inquisitive nature, the questions, the cheek, the heartbreaking smiles.

It wasn't even as if anything had really happened between her and Giovanni. Not really. Just a few kisses. But the urge to be around him was strong. Stronger than she'd ever experienced before. And the pull to be around Sofia was strong too. They were a partnership—a pair—and she couldn't think of them any other way. And that didn't terrify her quite the way it had before.

She pulled her diary from her bag and glanced at the dates. Depending on how things went with Grace and Hope, she could be here for another three weeks. If things stayed steady, maybe another five. No one could predict when the twins would need to be delivered. There was a good chance that the surgery Lizzy and Leon had performed could result in premature labour for Gabrielle.

Autumn pushed her diary deep back inside her bag, trying not to think about how that could turn out.

She reached the café and saw Lizzy sitting inside, out of the morning sun.

'Hey...' She smiled as she sat down beside her.

Lizzy had three drinks in front of her. Iced water, a pot of tea, and a diet soda. She gave Autumn a smile. 'Sorry, I couldn't decide, and as soon as I sat down I decided not to wait.'

Autumn grinned at Lizzy's protruding stomach. 'How many weeks are you now?' She looked up as the waiter approached and ordered a cappuccino and some toast.

Lizzy rubbed her belly. 'Only twenty weeks.

But I feel much bigger than I actually am. I think it's just the heat in Rome right now. It's killing me.'

Autumn gave a nod and went for a careful question. 'So, how're things with you and Leon?'

Lizzy looked at her. 'I take it you know it's Leon's baby?'

Autumn nodded again. 'I had heard that.'

'Well, it's true.' There was a gleam in her eye and she leaned across the table to Autumn. 'I'll tell you how things are with me and Leon if you tell me what's going on with you and Giovanni.'

Autumn sagged back in her chair and let out a brief laugh. 'I wouldn't know where to start.'

Lizzy took a sip of one of her drinks, tucked a strand of blonde hair behind her ear and gave Autumn a thoughtful look. 'Okay, then, I'll start. I met Leon at med school in New York years ago. We were together then, and at the end I went back to Australia and he went back to Italy. We met again at a conference a few months ago and this…' she gestured down her stomach '…is the result.'

'Wow.' Autumn knew that her eyes had widened at this succinct sum-up.

'It's okay,' said Lizzy, waving her hand as the waitress arrived with Autumn's order. 'Go on—ask the million questions that just jumped into your head.' She bent forward and grabbed a piece of Autumn's toast from the plate. 'That's as long as you don't mind sharing with a pregnant woman.' She gave Autumn a wink. 'When it suits me, I'm eating for two.'

Autumn pushed the whipped butter towards her. 'Go ahead. I'm still in shock.'

'That's okay.' Lizzy smiled. 'I tend to have that effect on people these days. Give me a moment... I can probably shock you some more.'

'So, is Leon okay about the baby?'

Lizzy wrinkled her nose as she spread butter on the toast. 'Here's the thing: I've known him a long time. Leon never wanted kids. I knew that. And, to be honest, neither did I. This wasn't planned in any way, but...' She let her voice trail off for a second, as if she was deciding what to say next. 'For me, having our baby was the only option. Still, I struggled with how I felt about it all. Then I got the invitation to take part in the surgery. I knew I couldn't say no, and I knew it would give me a chance to be in the same room with Leon again and tell him we'd made a baby.'

Autumn shook her head in amazement. 'You make it all sound so simple.'

Lizzy let out a deep laugh. 'Oh, believe me, it's anything but simple. But if I say it out loud that way it keeps all my emotions in check.' She took a bite of her toast.

'Do you need to keep your emotions in check?'

As soon as the words were out of her mouth Autumn regretted them. The question was too personal.

But Lizzy answered in an instant. 'I did. But things have kind of turned around.'

She held out her hand. Autumn gave a gasp in surprise. A sparkling princess cut aquamarine with a diamond-encrusted band. It was stunning. She hadn't even noticed. 'You're engaged?'

Lizzy beamed at her. 'Told you I'd shock you again. Engaged and getting married at some point soon. It was a difficult road, but we got there. And I can't tell you how happy I am.' She took another bite of toast. 'Now, enough about me—let's give my pregnancy hormones a break. What about you? What's going on with you and Giovanni?'

Autumn gulped down some coffee, scalding the back of her throat and choking. She was still getting over the engagement bombshell. But Lizzy did look well and truly happy.

Lizzy laughed. 'That'll teach you to stall.'

Heat rushed into Autumn's cheeks. She liked this Australian woman, and it seemed that she'd got the kind of happy-ever-after that people liked to dream of. But she'd been honest. She'd said it hadn't been easy. And that made Autumn feel more comfortable around her. It wasn't as if there were many people to have a heart-to-heart with around here, and Lizzy was definitely her best bet. It was time to let out everything that was jumbling around in her brain.

'I kissed him…' she groaned.

Lizzy leaned forward again, snatching the second piece of toast. 'Really? When?'

'Two weeks ago. He took me shopping, then he took me to a rooftop bar that has views of the Colosseum. We kissed as the sun was setting.'

Lizzy gave a low whistle. 'Way to knock it out of the park with the romantic movie setting.'

Autumn shook her head. 'But since then nothing. I just don't know what's happening.'

'I could have matched you there for weeks!'

Autumn laughed. 'It's ridiculous. I'm only here for a short spell. Once the surgery is over, I'll head back to London. And he's got a kid, and I'm not sure I'm the kid type.' She put her hand over her mouth. 'Oops.'

It was too late. She stopped talking before she got herself into more trouble.

Lizzy didn't look hurt by the comment. She looked thoughtful. 'Kids aren't for everyone. I had to think long and hard about it.' She put her hand across the table and rested it on Autumn's. 'And it's fine for you to say that.'

'But I don't really know.' Autumn sighed as she lowered her head onto her other hand. 'And that's what's wrong. Does he even like me? Does he think of me that way? I've never really taken the time to consider kids in my life. And now I've met this dreamy guy, with eyes that just make me shudder, and a little girl who I think is great, and all I can see for myself is a whole lot of hurt.'

Lizzy pulled her hand back and folded her arms. 'Okay... Don't tell me you're one of those *I don't deserve nice things* kind of gals?'

Autumn gave a short laugh. 'No, not really. I'm just scared I'll do or say something wrong while I'm trying to work out things in my head. I think his sister already hates me.'

'Does Sofia like you?'

'Well, yes, I think so.'

Lizzy shrugged. 'Well, that's all that matters. She's Giovanni's world. And I can already tell that he likes you. Maybe he's worried about some of the same kind of things that you are.'

Lizzy waved her arm and ordered more toast. And some cakes.

'I need to talk to him,' said Autumn softly.

'Yes, you do,' agreed Lizzy. 'And I had to do exactly the same thing.' She paused and wrinkled her nose. 'But why is it so hard?' She tilted her head to the side. 'I forgot to check—how was the kiss?'

Autumn groaned again and shook her head.

'That good? Darn it, I should have ordered even more food. We might be here for a while…'

CHAPTER EIGHT

THE GIRLS WERE at twenty-nine weeks. He'd started calling them that in his head, because Autumn was using the term more and more. It was like a term of affection. More personal than 'the twins'. Their heart surgery had been performed three weeks ago now, and there were no signs of imminent labour.

When they talked about the girls to their teams, they used the names chosen by Gabrielle and Matteo. It was Team Hope and Team Grace.

Giovanni and Autumn had finally chosen their teams after a little bit of cat-and-mouse games. It had been fun. They'd debated over a few members. Autumn had been fair. She had a wide team, with the skill-set she needed along with younger team members who would have a chance to learn and gain from the experience. It was a good mix.

Their longest debate had been over whether a certain team member was up to the job. Autumn had delicately raised a few issues about his suitability and Giovanni's first reaction had been to be instantly defensive of the person in question—he'd worked with him for years and liked him. It had taken him a few days to realise that Autumn was being far more objective than him. She'd seen things he'd been blind to and had excused. It wasn't that the person couldn't do his job, it was more that he shouldn't be doing *this* job.

It seemed Autumn Fraser kept surprising him time and time again.

The clinical training room was warm. It was as if the hospital's air-conditioning was objecting to having to work so hard. There were six different things happening at once—six teams all performing their own part of the procedure.

Tempers were fraying, and when he saw a scalpel hit a wall in frustration, Giovanni clapped his hands above his head.

'Enough. Everyone—time out. It's too warm. You've all been working extremely long hours. Unless you have immediate clinical duties, I want you to get out of here for the next few hours. We'll start fresh tomorrow morning. Seven a.m.'

Autumn pulled her hair from the nape of her neck and stretched out her back, giving him a silent nod.

There were a few stunned faces. Glances were exchanged. But eventually the room filled with the sound of surgical gloves being snapped off and the clink of instruments being put back on trays.

Slowly but surely the tired and various levels of sweaty staff all filed out of the room.

Autumn leaned on the wall and folded her arms. 'Should we be concerned?'

Giovanni moved across the room, pulling his surgical cap from his head. Every muscle in his body ached. 'Should we be concerned that our staff are so focused on these surgeries that they've forgotten how to take care of themselves or each other?'

She must be tired too—although he knew she would never admit it.

'There's one more job still to do today,' she said.

His brain started automatically filtering all his tasks for the patients he currently had. He never usually missed anything. 'What is it?' he asked, his brow creasing.

Autumn pulled her pale pink scrub top away from her chest, letting it flap for a few moments. 'The most important thing.' She had a smile in her eyes.

'Tell me.'

He was getting annoyed with himself now.

What he really wanted to do was pull his own scrub top entirely over his head. Watching her flap her own to let the air circulate was giving him glimpses of pale skin that were more than a little distracting.

'Sofia. I need to take her stitches out today.'

She laughed at the expression he clearly had on his face right now. It had gone clean out of his head. His own daughter. He'd checked her dressing every day. Only cleaning and redressing when he felt it was necessary. The wound seemed to have healed well—due, of course, to the skill of the person who'd done the stitches.

Autumn's hand went into the pocket of her scrubs. 'She texted me. Didn't you know that?'

'What?' Sofia didn't have a phone. Which could only mean one thing...

He pulled his own phone from his pocket and scrolled down. His hand went to his head. *Oh, no.*

Autumn threw back her head and laughed. 'Your face! It's fine. I knew straight away it wasn't you. And—to be fair—she didn't pretend to be you.'

He read the messages quickly. His heart-rate started to slow from its panicked state. Then he got to the end and his eyebrows shot skyward.

He looked up and saw Autumn was nodding

her head and smiling at him. 'I see you've made me a promise. I expect you to see it through.'

It was clear from the text conversation that Sofia wanted them to spend more time together. She'd promised Autumn that Giovanni would take them both to a favourite place of hers.

Papà and me take you here.

'Where's "here"?' he asked.

She shrugged. 'I think the picture she meant to send got lost somewhere along the line. Where do you think it is?'

'I have no idea.' Then he stopped and put his hands on his hips. 'Wait—was Sofia wanting me to take you to a place she loves, or a place you want to see?'

Autumn shook her head. 'She's five, and her English is great, but honestly we didn't type that many words.'

Of course. Giovanni bowed his head, trying not to laugh out loud. He sometimes overestimated his daughter's abilities.

He gave a solemn nod. 'In that case I'm going to make a few presumptions. I think Sofia was saying we'd take you somewhere, and as the father of a five-year-old I'm assuming it's a place that she loves.' He met her green gaze. 'And I know exactly where that might be.'

The expression on her face told him that she was intrigued, and he decided not to give the secret away.

The more time he spent around this woman, the more time he *wanted* to spend around her. His sister Eleonora had asked a million questions about Autumn—some of which he hadn't been able to answer. And that annoyed him. He wanted to know more. He wanted to know everything about her. But that thought overwhelmed him.

Sofia had spent the last week talking about Autumn. He shouldn't be surprised that his daughter had decided to use his phone. She was bright. He was just glad that Autumn had realised immediately that it was Sofia.

'How about we get changed and I'll take Sofia's stitches out this afternoon?'

He gave an immediate nod. 'Sure—thank you.' Then he paused a second. 'Let me check on a couple of patients and I'll meet you outside the locker rooms in half an hour.'

'No problem.'

Half an hour later Autumn was standing outside the locker room in the softly draped green dress that clung to her curves. That had been his immediate thought when he'd saw her try it on in the shop. But now, up close, he saw the best thing about this dress was the way it brought out the colour in her emerald eyes.

'Something wrong?' she asked.

He blinked and shook his head. 'No—sorry, lost in thought. Let's go.'

They headed outside to his car, and as he drove through the streets he realised this was the first time that Autumn would see his home.

His skin prickled, and he felt oddly nervous as he wondered if he'd left socks or shirts lying in places he shouldn't. Giovanni generally kept a relatively tidy house. But because his time was split between work and Sofia he didn't often have visitors, so didn't think much about how ready his house was for visitors.

As they pulled up outside the private gates of his villa on the outskirts of Rome, Autumn gave a light laugh as he pressed a button for them to open.

'Nice.' She glanced around the private neighbourhood. All the houses had similar gates and grounds. 'Do you talk to your neighbours around here?'

He moved the car up the paved driveway to the front door and the gates closed behind them. 'I know some of them,' he said with a shrug. 'Others keep to themselves.'

'And you?'

He blinked, thinking about his answer. The

truth was he pretty much kept to himself too. Some of the surrounding neighbours had known Anna. He didn't really want to have conversations with them about her or be reminded of how much other people had found her to be a shining light. Or see the sympathy in their eyes when they looked at him.

He didn't need pity. He and Sofia were doing fine. At least he'd always thought they were. But his connection and chemistry with Autumn was making him ask himself questions he wasn't sure he knew the answers to.

Autumn opened the car door and stepped out, clearly admiring the ochre and pale orange villa. 'Have you lived here long?'

'A few years. I had an apartment in Rome to begin with, but when Anna was expecting we moved here.'

He saw Autumn swallow, and realised he was taking another woman into the home he'd shared with his wife. She wasn't to know that all his memories weren't good ones. Maybe, because of their kiss, she was feeling intimidated. He hated the thought of that.

'Come,' he said quickly. 'I'll show you around. Sofia will be dropped here from school in a few minutes.'

He opened the door and led her into the wide

cream hallway. Giving her a guided tour only took a few minutes. The villa had four bedrooms, a study, two bathrooms and a kitchen and living room with glass doors looking out over a spacious garden. The doors took up the complete back wall of the house.

Autumn gave a broad smile as she stepped into the room. He pressed a button for the doors to concertina back.

'Oh, wow. This is like something you see in those TV shows. You know…the ones where people are trying to decide if they want to live in another country?' Then she gave a short laugh. 'And, of course, the presenters show them something they fall in love with that's *way* outside their budget.'

He laughed too. 'Of course.' Then he glanced around in surprise. He'd never thought of his home like that. 'These doors weren't here initially. I had them put in a few years ago.' He rolled his eyes. 'Sofia was a toddler at the time, and no matter how many times she was told to stay away from the building work…'

Autumn nodded, getting it immediately. 'You needed twenty sets of eyes in the back of your head?'

'Fifty.'

The doors were wide now, and a gentle breeze

blew in, bringing in scents of evergreen, wisteria, azaleas and poppies.

'Coffee?' he asked, standing in front of his machine.

Autumn turned and walked over, running her hand along the countertop. 'You could fit my whole flat back in London into this big room. It's amazing.' She touched the silver machine, with its array of buttons and steam wand. 'You don't like to do things by halves, do you?'

He gave a pleased shrug as he lifted cups from the cupboard. Autumn made her selection of coffee and then walked outside to the garden. Humming to herself, she walked around touching a few bushes and flowers, then sat down at the table on the patio outside.

He carried out the cups. 'I have to admit I was a bit worried about what we might find when we got here.'

She laughed and shook her head. 'Well, I can assure you I don't have any right to comment. I can tell you exactly what you'll find back at my hotel room. Toothpaste on the sink and a pile of clothes on a chair that I should have sent to the laundry today.' She shook her head. 'No judgement here. In fact, I'm really impressed.'

'I'm relieved. Sofia can be a one-girl destruction module when she wants to be. I have a woman who comes in to help out a few times a week, but sometimes Sofia wreaks havoc just after she leaves.'

'Papà!'

Right on cue, Sofia came running through the main door and into the back room. Her eyes lit up like saucers once she realised Autumn was there too, and Giovanni's heart soared.

'You came! You got my message!'

Autumn grinned. 'Yes, I got your message. Of course I came.'

Sofia threw her bag onto the sofa and continued to barrel out, almost straight onto Autumn's lap.

He saw Autumn look back through the house and realised she was wondering who had dropped Sofia off. 'My sister,' he said, then clarified when he saw the widening of Autumn's eyes. 'Bella. She's working this evening, so she'll only come in if there's an issue. If my car is here, she knows I'm home and she can just drop Sofia and go.'

He could almost see her sigh of relief. 'Just how hard a time did Eleonora give you?'

Autumn shook her head. 'It's nothing…she was fine.' But she gave him a sideways glance. 'Just a little scary.'

He laughed and leaned forward. 'Does it help if I tell you she scares me too?'

Autumn took a sip of her coffee, and the smile

she gave him reached up into her eyes. 'Absolutely.' She turned around to give Sofia her full attention. 'Well, Ms Lombardi, are you ready to get your stitches out?'

Sofia nodded and Giovanni stood automatically. 'Let me collect what you'll need. Autumn, you know where the bathroom is so you can wash your hands.'

Five minutes later he'd opened a stitch removal pack on the carefully sterilised table. Autumn spoke gently to Sofia. 'I'm just going to remove this dressing. It might feel a little tuggy while I take it off. There. Good girl.'

The wound was tight, and a tiny bit red around the stitches, as if they could have been removed already. Her body was ready for them to be gone.

Autumn's face was right in front of Sofia's. 'I will have these out in a few moments. You just have to hold still. Do you want to stay standing—or do you want to sit on your *papà*'s lap?'

He could see the flicker on Sofia's face and resisted the temptation to automatically pull her into his arms. He had to let her choose for herself, and from the determined set of her jaw he knew exactly what she would say.

'I can stand here. I'm a brave girl.'

'Yes, you are.' Autumn nodded solemnly. 'Then give me a moment.'

She was good. She was very good. Autumn removed the stitches in literally the blink of an eye.

'You're finished?' asked Sofia in amazement.

'All done.' Autumn smiled, disposing of the tools and snapping off her gloves.

Giovanni leaned forward to look at the thin line on his daughter's upper arm. Autumn's prediction had been correct. The scar was neat and well-healed and it would fade with age. In a few years it would be barely noticeable at all.

'I don't think you need to cover it now,' said Autumn. 'Just try not to get into any more fights.'

Sofia dipped her head, looking sorry for all of two seconds before a grin lit up her face again and she clapped her hands. 'Now we can go to my favourite place!' She turned to Giovanni. 'Can't we, Papà? I promised we would.'

He raised his eyebrows. '*You* promised that we would on *my* phone.'

'You weren't using it,' she replied brightly. 'You were in the shower.'

Autumn gave him a knowing smile. 'No secrets here, right?'

He tried his best not to rise to the bait and turned his full attention back on his daughter. 'You know you're not supposed to use Papà's phone without permission?'

Sofia looked innocent. It seemed as though his daughter had mastered that art from birth. 'You were in the shower. I couldn't ask. And I didn't want Autumn to forget to take out my stitches.' She said it so matter-of-factly that he almost wondered what point he'd been trying to make.

He sighed and leaned back in his chair. 'Okay, tell me where you want us to take Autumn.'

'The pyramid!' she exclaimed.

Of course. Just as he had suspected.

'There's a pyramid in Rome?' Autumn looked amazed.

Giovanni nodded. 'The Pyramid of Cestius. It's Sofia's favourite place.'

Autumn's eyes were sparkling. 'Is that where we're going?'

'As long as you want to.'

'Of course! I can't wait. I had no idea there was a pyramid in Rome.'

Giovanni made a quick call, and then it took ten minutes to get Sofia changed and all of them into the car. They drove for another forty-five minutes to reach Via Raffaele Persichetti.

Autumn hadn't believed him when he'd said there was a pyramid until she actually saw the monument.

He parked the car and they walked up to it.

Sofia raced ahead. The little girl could barely contain her excitement.

This afternoon had been illuminating. Autumn had seen around his home. He'd given her a whistle-stop tour of everything: the four bedrooms—Sofia's had a large bookcase crammed with books and the room that was clearly Giovanni's had rumpled navy bedding but was surprisingly tidy—the bathrooms, his study, and finally the kitchen and living space.

She'd felt a little nervous, but the house was breathtaking. It didn't have the feel of a pristine show house. It was warmer than that. Elements of Giovanni and Sofia were scattered around the house, but Autumn hadn't felt overwhelmed by the presence of another woman. There had been one photograph on a small corner table that she assumed was of Sofia and her mother, but it wasn't prominently displayed. Autumn had felt comfortable.

The glass doors and the garden had taken her breath away. It was amazing that leaving the busy heart of Rome behind could reveal such a green and tranquil space. Her heart had been struck by how impersonal her own home was back in London. Sure, she'd barely lived in it for the last twelve months, but even before then had it really felt like home?

She looked sideways at Giovanni. He had his

hands in his trouser pockets as they climbed the hill, the warm breeze ruffling his dark hair. Her stomach gave a little flip. What was she more scared of? The possibility of a relationship with him and his daughter, or the possibility that he might not want that at all?

She had to find out.

She swallowed, ignoring how dry her throat felt, and glanced at the monument they were approaching. 'Why on earth is there a pyramid in Rome?' she asked.

'Because I wanted one!' shouted Sofia, spinning around with her hands in the air.

Giovanni laughed, and when he spoke his voice was low. 'Despite what my daughter says, this pyramid has been here a lot longer than she has. Most people think pyramids are only in Egypt, Mexico or India. This is the only ancient pyramid in Europe.' He held his hand out towards it. 'This pyramid is over two thousand years old and was built as a tomb for Gaius Cestius, a Roman senator and general.'

'How high is it?' asked Autumn as she stared upwards. The sun was glinting off the white marble slabs on the outside of the pyramid.

'It's over thirty-five metres.'

'We can go inside.' Sofia had appeared, and she was looking around, making sure no one could hear her.

'We can?' Autumn was surprised.

Giovanni nodded. 'Yes, it's open to the public. Usually only a few Saturdays a month, but I gave a friend a call and he said it's fine for us to look inside today.'

They walked around to an entrance on the far side. Autumn shot him a curious look. 'Do you have friends everywhere?'

He gave her a sideways glance. 'I've looked after a lot of patients. And patients have families.'

She understood instantly. He wouldn't give her details. A doctor would never break patient confidentiality. And not every patient story had a good outcome—Autumn knew that. But whoever this family member was, and however they had met Giovanni, it was clear they were willing to do him a favour.

As they neared the entrance Giovanni pointed to two spots on the ground. 'They did some excavations here in the sixteen-hundreds. They think the pyramid was originally in the countryside, but as Rome grew it became surrounded by other buildings. An enclosure, columns, other tombs… They found two marble bases with fragments of the bronze statues that once stood on them.'

Autumn stopped and took a deep breath, looking all around her. Rome stretched for miles. She shook her head. 'To think this was once the countryside,' she said in wonder. 'How on earth has it survived when so much else has been lost?' Then she laughed, 'Of course you have the Colosseum, and so much else in Rome. You seem especially good at looking after your famous artefacts.'

Giovanni held out his hands. 'It's not clear now, but this used to stand at the fork between two ancient roads. It was incorporated into part of the city's fortifications, which is probably why it's still here today.'

She loved this. She actually *loved* this. Exploring a part of the city she'd likely never have found for herself, with two guides who were enthusiastic and enjoyable to be around.

Sofia bounded up. 'Come inside,' she pleaded, tugging at Autumn's hand.

It was like a warm wrap of wool winding its way around her heart. The heat. The warmth. The look in Sofia's eyes. The way her heart expanded in her chest. It wasn't just Autumn's hand Sofia was tugging at…

Tears pricked in her eyes. The overwhelming surge was unexpected. She blinked the tears away. 'Of course. I'd love to.'

She stepped inside the quiet space. There wasn't much to see, but it wasn't a visual experience—it was a completely sensory one. Both Sofia and Giovanni seemed to know this, and they both stood quietly beside her, letting her breathe in the cool air around them.

The inside of the pyramid wasn't large—and it wasn't entirely what she'd expected. It was a barrel-vaulted cavity. The inside walls were light. It was apparent that at one point there had been frescoes, but only a few scant traces remained—just a couple of angels in the curve of the ceiling. There might not be much to see, but the room was filled with reverence. The city noise outside just appeared to fade away. The room was silent. But nothing about it was creepy.

Autumn rubbed her arms. Sofia was staring happily around, as if she enjoyed the quiet of the place too. Every step echoed. This had been the resting place for someone for years before it was plundered. She closed her eyes for a moment.

'You okay?' An arm slid around her waist and Giovanni's lips brushed against her ear as he whispered.

Her hand rested over his. 'Yes,' she said quietly. 'Just taking myself back in time and wondering what this might have looked like two thousand years ago.'

The heat from his body was comforting in this cool air. She was happy to stay resting next to him. But then a little voice interrupted them.

'I've got a drawing in my room. I can show you what it looked like.'

She smiled and looked down, Sofia's eyes were bright with excitement. She knelt down. 'I would love to see that. I bet it's perfect.'

Giovanni's hand squeezed her shoulder in support. He was letting this happen. He was letting her get close to his daughter. That filled her with a happiness she couldn't even have imagined.

Her brain jumped to a million possibilities and a billion conversations they hadn't even touched on. She had to take her time. Think about this carefully. There was a little girl right in front of her who wore her heart on her sleeve, and Autumn was beginning to wonder if she did too.

She stood up and turned to face Giovanni, aware of how close they were. 'Thank you for bringing me here,' she said with a smile on her face. 'I really appreciate it.'

For a moment all she could see was his dark brown eyes, so deep they almost seemed to pull her straight in. She'd never been much of a romantic. She'd never really had the big romance dream. But something pinged in her head. For her, this look felt like the one she'd seen exchanged between her friends at their wedding. And while this flooded her with happiness, there was still a tiny element of panic in her veins.

She knew exactly how she felt right now. What she didn't know was how Giovanni felt.

She wanted to go with her gut and imagine that he was in exactly the same place as her. That would make her feel safe. Sure, it would open up a whole world of questions about her job, her life and her future plans. It would also challenge her to wonder if she could ever let go of her whole self and let someone else have her heart.

She so, so hoped he was in the same place as her.

But did she know that for sure?

Giovanni blinked and the edges of his lips turned upwards. Even though the air was cool, she just wanted to melt. This was it. This was what she'd been looking for.

'Giovanni—' she started, but a voice cut in behind them.

'We have to close now.'

She spun round, her heart sinking deep inside her. The man gave Giovanni a nod and he held out his hand to Sofia.

The moment was gone—wrenched away—and Autumn struggled to catch her breath. Which was ridiculous, and she knew that.

'Will you come and see my pictures?' Sofia was skipping along as they exited the pyramid.

'Of course.' Her response was automatic.

Giovanni gave a nod. 'Shall we pick up something for dinner?'

She smiled, her head spinning. What she probably needed to do was go back to her hotel room and try to get her head straight. But her conversation with Lizzy was pushing her forward. She knew there was a chance here to have the talk with Giovanni that she needed to have. The chance to find out if he might want to take things a stage further.

The thought of being shot down in flames danced around her brain. She was pretty sure her adrenalin rates were currently topping out at their max. But she was an adult. She could do this. She could have this conversation and deal with the consequences.

Or not…

CHAPTER NINE

IT WAS LATE. Pizza had been eaten. Pictures had been shown. And Sofia had finally gone to bed.

The sun had disappeared in the sky and they were still sitting in his garden, drinking wine. The white fairy lights that Sofia had insisted they wind around the trees were twinkling in the dimming sky.

Autumn was looking like the most perfect woman in the world right now. But she lived in another country. She probably had career plans he didn't even know about. Could he really take the next step?

As he watched she lifted her wine glass to her pink lips and took another sip.

Every now and then her gaze met his, then flickered away. It was as if she wanted to say something but couldn't quite get up the nerve.

A feeling he recognised.

Giovanni wasn't sure where to start. Or if he should even start. All he knew was that if he was contemplating starting a new relationship that would involve his child, he wanted to be up-front right from the start. It seemed like the only way.

He reached for the wine bottle to top up her glass.

'You'd better stop doing that,' she said, in an oh-so-soft voice.

'Why?'

'Because I'm a lightweight. It only takes a couple of glasses for me to start to feel drunk.'

Giovanni picked up the remote on the table and flicked a button, turning music on around them.

Soft jazz sounds filled the air.

Autumn started laughing.

'You don't like my music?'

She shook her head. 'It's just the fact you have all this!' She flung her arms wide. 'This! This amazing house and even more amazing garden. Lights strung between the trees and speakers hidden in the bushes…' She raised her eyebrows. 'All these belonging to a man who masquerades as a master surgeon.'

He stood up and pulled her up next to him, wrapping his arms around her as he started swaying to the music. 'May I have this dance?' he asked, his voice low.

Her hands rested on his shoulders. 'If you must.'

Her head was against his chest, her gaze on the table. 'What are you looking at?'

Sofia had left her pictures on the table. She'd brought them from her room earlier, to show Autumn.

'Her pictures.' Her voice was quiet. 'The pyramid. The pyramid with a dinosaur. The dinosaur with a clown. And the space rocket with a hot air balloon.' She lifted her head and blinked heavy-lidded eyes at him. 'How do you manage to keep it all straight in your head?'

He frowned. 'Keep what straight?'

'The crazy kid stuff?'

'Sofia's not crazy.' He laughed softly.

She pulled back and looked up at him. 'Sofia is a delight,' she said flatly. 'But…' She leaned over and grabbed one of the pictures. It was another one of clowns. But they all had sad faces and glittery green shoes. 'How do you deal with this? How do you know if she's up or down? How do you know how to react?'

His chest tightened a little. 'Autumn, not every sad picture is a trauma reveal. Sometimes kids feel a bit sad. I let Sofia paint whatever she wants. That's what being a parent is. How on earth do I explain a clown and a stegosaurus holding hands when a stegosaurus doesn't even have hands? It doesn't always mean something. She enjoys painting, drawing, and generally getting glitter all over my house. Don't you remember tramping in dirt from outside? Drawing on the walls in your room? Climbing out of windows or up trees?'

When he caught the expression on her face he leaned back, moving his hands from her waist to her upper arms.

'Autumn, didn't you ever just play as a child? Do crazy things? Build a den where you weren't supposed to? Eat berries from a bush when you had no idea what they were?'

She looked so horrified that he knew the answer instantly.

'Why would you do things like that?' she asked in a small voice.

He reached up and stroked a strand of hair away from her face. 'Because that's what children do. It's normal play. And it's part of the heart failure of being a parent.'

She shuddered, and when she blinked he could see her eyes were wet. 'But doesn't every single second of that terrify you?' she whispered.

He could see the hairs on her arms standing on end. Now, he was really beginning to understand about her interest in trauma. She'd said her parents had never been bad to her—and he knew that she believed that. But didn't she know about the impact of constant controlling behaviour and its lasting effects? Because from where he was standing, she was living proof of that.

He took a deep breath and felt something fill his heart. He loved this woman. He wanted to take care of her, protect her. She was a good and true person. But could he take on someone with obvious lasting damage without worrying about her impact on Sofia?

'Autumn, you should know that when Sofia was a newborn I didn't sleep for weeks. I was a physical wreck. I used to hold a mirror in front of her face to make sure she was breathing. I actually thought I was losing it. Both Anna and I were the same.' He gave a sad smile. 'It wasn't until *much* later that I found out that lots of people do that. Most people are overwhelmed by their first kid and that whole new element of things being out of their control. Talking to others made me realise I was just a normal new parent. Not the person who was losing all reality and rational thought that I feared I was becoming.'

She took a few deep breaths, the expression on her face thoughtful. 'And once Sofia got older?'

He swung one hand towards the glass doors. 'I told you—when she was a toddler, I was in the middle of renovations and I was on my own. Sofia had an absolute gift of being where she shouldn't be. There wasn't a child gate in the world she couldn't get through.'

Autumn shook her head, the deepening sunset silhouetting her in shades of orange and red.

'But how on earth did you cope?'

'I took it one day at a time. That's all you can do. And I asked for help when I needed it.' He chose his next words carefully. 'Part of being a child is making mistakes and learning. It's my job to keep her safe to the best of my ability. But no matter how hard I wish for that to happen, there are always things I can't foresee.' He gave a shrug. 'Look at what happened at school the other day.'

'Yes…'

Her voice was quiet and he could tell she was still thinking. 'Autumn, how much of a childhood did you have?'

She gave a little jerk and stared at him. 'What does that mean?'

Giovanni could sense her automatic defences slipping into place. He reached up and slid his hand into her hair. He kept his voice low. 'I mean that I have a woman in front of me I'm very attracted to. She's a brilliant surgeon, with a brilliant mind and a big heart.' He moved his hand and ran one finger lightly down her cheek. 'But sometimes she seems a little sad. As if she's never had the chance to live a crazy life and do things that seem stupid.'

Her gaze met his. 'But...do people *have* to do that?'

He ran his fingertip over her lips. 'Only if they want to. And I want you to know that if you ever feel like you want to be a bit crazy and lose control, I'm your man. I'll take your hand and show you how.'

A tear slid down her cheek and he resisted the urge to brush it away, wondering if Autumn had ever had a conversation like this before. Inside, he knew that she hadn't.

She gave a small shake of her head. 'What if it feels like too much? What if I just want to take baby steps?'

Regret flooded through him. He was losing his heart to someone who might never be able to lose her heart to him. She was too closed-off. Too focused on control. Was he making a mistake?

'I'd say that baby steps are a start,' he whispered.

'Good.'

She slid her hands around his neck, standing on tiptoes and brushing her lips against his. Part of his brain was screaming at him. Telling him to be cautious. But his body had other ideas and he matched every move that she made.

Within a few moments he was frustrated by the confines of her dress, and he pulled back and held his hand out to hers. The message was clear. But he wanted her to be sure of their next move.

Her hand slid into his and they walked back into the house and into his bedroom.

Giovanni took a few seconds to go and check on Sofia. By the time he got back to his own room Autumn's dress was on the floor.

That was all he needed. He stopped thinking about everything else. He pushed it all away. Autumn was standing in her underwear, smiling at him. Her green eyes were still bright in the dim lights. She'd never looked more beautiful or more sure about anything.

She gave a smile and held out her hand. 'What are you waiting for? Let's try some baby steps.'

And he kicked his bedroom door closed behind him.

CHAPTER TEN

HE'D SLEPT WITH AUTUMN. And relived the experience a few times since. He'd brought another woman into his home, slept with her in that home, while his daughter was in the house.

If someone had asked him a few months ago about starting a new relationship he would have told them he had a whole set of rules. Those rules involved a certain length of time spent getting to know her, a judgement call over if she should meet Sofia, then the possibility of taking the relationship further—in the first instance far away from his family home.

But Autumn seemed to have thrown all that out of the window for him.

And he couldn't quite get his brain around it.

'You did *what*?'

He'd just confessed all to his sister, Bella. She was just as feisty as Eleanor, but easier to talk to.

'I know,' he muttered, pacing in front of the windows of his office.

'She must be something special.'

'She is.' Giovanni's shoulders sagged a little with the admission.

'So, what's wrong?'

'Who said something was wrong?'

'You did. As soon as you picked up the phone to me. You don't *do* this, Giovanni.' Bella knew him too well.

He leaned against the wall. 'I feel dishonest. She's let me know that she has issues with control. All related to how she was brought up.'

'Issues that mean your relationship won't work?'

He could hear the concern in Bella's tone. 'No, or maybe yes. I don't know.' He let out a giant sigh. 'She's terrified about things being out of her control. Even the whole child thing terrifies her. I don't think she realises just how good she is around Sofia. Or how good she is with the babies in ICU. The staff there love her.'

'Wait—I'm not really getting this.'

Giovanni rolled his eyes. 'Neither am I. I can't quite work things out.'

'Okay, tell me the problem from your side.'

Giovanni nodded and started walking again. 'Okay, I haven't really told her about Anna.'

There was a long silence. Then, 'She doesn't know you were married?' Bella sounded confused.

'No, no—she knows that. She just doesn't know that things weren't that great with Anna.'

'You told her about the accident?'

He stopped pacing again. 'Yes, she knows about that. But, like everyone else in the hospital, she thinks that Anna and I were...' His voice tailed off.

'Still completely in love?'

Giovanni's stomach clenched. 'Yes.'

'And why is that such a bad thing? Why do you need to tell her anything at all? Let her have the same impression as most people—that your beloved wife died and you've been a widower these last four years.'

Giovanni froze. 'But that's wrong,' he said deeply.

'Explain why.'

Giovanni ran his fingers through his hair. 'Because if I'm starting a new relationship I want to be honest from the start. I don't want to throw it in later. I want to sit down and tell Autumn that things weren't that great between Anna and me. That I think she probably wanted to leave anyway, long before the accident. And that I'm not even one hundred per cent sure it even was an accident.'

'Giovanni...?'

Bella's voice was full of concern. And he knew he had to say more. 'I don't know. I'm probably just overthinking things. I mean, I'm ninety per cent sure it was an accident, but we had a fight just before she left. She was still on maternity leave. She shouldn't even have been travelling into work. But she told me she'd do anything to get out of the house and away from me. Said I was trapping her.'

Bella didn't speak for a few moments. It was clear she was taking all this in. She'd known Anna better than most.

When she spoke, her voice was steady. 'Giovanni, how long have you felt like this? Why didn't you tell me?'

Giovanni swallowed. 'Because I didn't want to admit it might be a possibility.'

'And it's not. You can't be rational about this. She was your wife, but you'd fallen out of love with each other. I *can* be rational. I knew you both. Anna was ready to leave. But she loved Sofia. She would never have done something like that. It was an accident. That's all it was. Just a damn stupid accident. Park those thoughts, Giovanni. You are not responsible for this in any way, shape or form.'

She paused and Giovanni didn't fill the silence. He was mulling over what Bella was saying. It felt as if an enormous cloud had lifted from his shoulders.

'It also tells me something else,' she said.

'What?'

'Just how much you like this new woman. It's only been—what? Five, six weeks? This is so unlike you. She's met Sofia, you've taken things further, and you want to tell her everything about you. Even your crazy fears that don't make sense. You know she has some issues herself and you're prepared to take them on board. Giovanni, you're making me think I should start to consider her as part of the family. She's special. You know she is.'

For the first time in the conversation the edges of Giovanni's lips moved upwards and his face broke into a smile. He nodded his head in agreement. 'You're right. She is.'

'Then whether you tell her you'd fallen out of love with your wife is entirely up to you. But focus on what you've got. This is the best news in the world for you and for Sofia. Take your chances, Giovanni. Grab them. If this is the woman you want in your life then work with her. Work together.'

The more Bella spoke, the lighter Giovanni felt. He should have spoken to her earlier. It would have helped him think things through.

'Thank you,' he said.

'Any time. I'm your sister. I love you. All I want for you and Sofia in this life is that you are both happy. And, Giovanni?'

'Yes?'

'Our whole family can love her just as much as you do.'

Relief flooded through him.

The phone line clicked and Giovanni turned and stared out at Rome. Their time was ticking down. They would be performing surgery any day now, and what then? What if, a few weeks after Hope and Grace were separated, Autumn was called elsewhere, to another surgery? How would he feel then?

He knew the answer to that already. And he didn't like it.

'Can we talk?'

Autumn lifted her head and broke into a smile when she saw Giovanni standing in her doorway. 'Sure—come on in.'

Her head had been spinning, partly from how their relationship had rapidly developed, and partly because of how much it filled her heart with joy.

She'd seen both Giovanni and Sofia the last two nights and, whilst part of her still had fears about letting go, she knew they were both stealing pieces of her heart. Which was why the large crease in Giovanni's brow now made her stomach clench.

He sat down opposite her.

'What's up?' She watched as he shifted on the chair and put his elbows on the table, leaning towards her.

'I wondered how you might be feeling about things.'

It was the first time she'd ever really heard Giovanni sound a bit nervous. Now it was her turn to shift uncomfortably. 'Feeling about what things?'

It was an idiotic response. She knew exactly what 'things' he was referring to. But right now she was trying to buy herself some time to think of the appropriate response. Because *I think I'm falling head over heels in love with you and your daughter and it completely terrifies me* probably wasn't the best response to give.

He licked his lips. He knew she was stalling. And that was probably worse.

'Do you plan to go back to London after the surgery? Or do you have another surgery lined up here?'

Okay. That sounded a bit easier to answer. Except it felt as if he was asking her what her intentions might be. Towards him and his daughter.

'I haven't made any plans,' she said quickly. 'I haven't been contacted about another surgery as yet. If things go well with Hope and Grace, I might go back to my place in London. I'm pretty much a free agent. I help out with general cases on a routine basis, but I can be called away at a moment's notice.'

Giovanni gave a slow, thoughtful nod, then his dark brown eyes met hers. 'Would you consider transferring your base to somewhere else?'

She knew she should say yes. Just about every pore in her body wanted to say yes. But the word stuck in her throat. Some people might call her crazy for considering upping sticks and moving her life and career to a new country, a new city, for a guy she'd only known for a few weeks.

Getting swept off her feet had never been Autumn Fraser's dream. In fact, she could almost feel the cells in her body panicking.

Giovanni's gaze was searing. The frown in his brow creased further and he leaned back in his chair. It wasn't hard for her to read what his concerns might be. He had Sofia to think of.

'I want to talk to you about something else,' he said gruffly. 'But maybe not.'

Before she had a chance to reply their pagers sounded simultaneously. Both them looked to their waists and then their gazes meshed.

'The girls,' they said in unison.

They both reached for the phone, but Giovanni

got there first, dialling a number and asking a few questions in rapid Italian.

'Eclampsia. We need to deliver the girls immediately. Lizzy and Leon are scrubbing in now.'

She was on her feet in an instant. 'They're only at thirty-one weeks. We'd hoped to get a bit longer.'

'We're lucky we got this long. Let's go.'

There was no time for anything else. Both wanted to watch the Caesarean section and be ready to take over the twins' care once they were out of the womb. It might be that the separation surgery would be required soon afterwards.

There was no time for this.

There was no time for them.

She wished she hadn't hesitated. She wished she'd reached out and grabbed him. But she just couldn't be that person. No matter how hard she tried.

Maybe it was time for a rethink.

CHAPTER ELEVEN

AUTUMN STOOD OVER the warming crib that held Grace and Hope. They were doing well. Although, to be honest, they had so many wires and monitors attached to them that it was virtually impossible to see any of their skin. But though they both had tiny knitted caps, and were obviously close together, Autumn could see their beautiful faces.

She pressed her lips together. The scan of the liver hadn't been great. In fact, it was going to require even more intense work than Autumn had planned for. The tiny blood vessels were so friable... She was actually scared.

Her skill as a surgeon had never been questioned. But now she was questioning it herself. Did she really have what it took to give Grace the life she deserved?

Her mind drifted to how comfortable the girls seemed. Neither of them had been upset or irritable since they'd been born. Breastfeeding was out of the question because of their positioning, and both currently had feeding tubes, but Gabrielle was hopeful that once her girls were separated, she would be able to breastfeed them both.

How much trauma was she about to cause these babies? It seemed alien to so many people, but was there a chance that separating them would do more harm than good?

Giovanni appeared at her side. 'I know what you're thinking.'

His voice was deep and low. She sighed, feeling his breath at the back of her neck. Things had been awkward this last week. There hadn't been time to sit down together and have the conversation that was badly needed. Both of them knew it wasn't the time.

There had been general agreement with all involved that they would allow Grace and Hope a few weeks of recovery time following the Caesarean section. Some time to establish their breathing, their feeding, and some time for Matteo and Gabrielle to get to know their daughters and to give the girls a chance to gain some strength for what lay ahead.

Autumn had spent hours here since they'd been born. Checking all the scan results, then rechecking them. She'd also spent hours in the clinical lab upstairs, practising surgeries.

'How do you know what I'm thinking?'

The tone of his voice held an edge of regret. 'Because I know you, Autumn. Better than you think. You're considering the surgery. You're thinking about childhood trauma.'

Her skin prickled and then she smiled. 'I am,' she said softly.

It felt good to know that someone could read her that well. She just wished she had the same confidence to know what Giovanni was thinking all the time.

She heard him suck in a deep breath.

'I think your work is excellent. I think it's really important,' he said. 'But have you ever asked yourself why it's an area of study you're interested in?'

She turned, automatically defensive. 'What do you mean?'

His fingers touched the bare skin on her arm. 'You know the lasting damage all types of childhood trauma can do. Physical, mental and emotional. It's the kind of trauma and behaviour that affects adults.'

'I know that.'

Her words were stiff. It was obvious he was trying to take her in a certain direction. But it was making her uncomfortable.

The look he gave her was full of sympathy and regret. 'Have you ever wondered why you find it so hard to give up control? To let go? To take a chance on giving a piece of your heart away—or even all of it?'

'You're saying I'm a victim of childhood trauma?' She could hear the indignant tone in her own voice. Tears pooled in her eyes.

He ran his fingers gently along her arm. 'You started this conversation with me some time ago. You told me your parents were never "bad" to you or your brother. But controlling behaviour can cause just as much damage as physical trauma. You must have thought about that sometimes, but I suspect you've just pushed it away.'

Autumn shook her head fiercely. 'This is ridiculous. Yes, they were controlling.' She put her hand to her chest. 'But me? I'm just me. Yes, I like to be in control of things. I don't like it when things happen that I can't plan for. That doesn't mean there's anything wrong with me. It's just who I am—and what's wrong with that?'

She stepped away from the warming crib and Grace and Hope. She was getting angry and irritated, and she didn't want anyone around to see two surgeons squabbling.

Giovanni ran his fingers through his hair. She could see the tiny lines around his eyes.

'I'm not saying there's anything wrong with you, Autumn. I just want you to understand how you got here.'

He put an arm around her waist and led her

out of the unit and to one of the windows in the nearby corridor. For the first time since she'd got here Rome was gloomy. The rain was lashing down on the streets outside and the clouds were low and grey.

'Have you ever gone outside and danced in the rain? Jumped in a fountain? Have you ever wanted to just turn up at the airport and pick the first flight that's available?'

She shook her head. None of those things were for her. The thought of turning up at an airport and getting a flight at random was ridiculous.

'Why would anyone do something like that? What if you've packed summer clothes and you end up on a flight to Iceland? Why wouldn't you want to plan your itinerary, get your currency in advance, know what you're going to do every day of your holiday? Time is too precious to waste.'

She saw his muscles tense. He closed his eyes for a second and she knew instantly that she'd disappointed him. This was why. This was why she'd tried to be so careful with her heart.

When he opened his eyes again, he gave a slow shake of his head. 'You are so right—time is too precious to waste. But what if, Autumn? What if my daughter hadn't looked at that screen of surgeons? What if she'd pointed to someone else? What if I'd called some other surgeon?'

Her skin chilled instantly.

'Some things are just random, Autumn. Some things—some meetings—are just happy mistakes. Or just darn good luck.'

She stared at him. Her head was flooding with thoughts. He could have picked someone else for this surgery. She'd still be back in London. In her flat. Alone. She'd never have met Giovanni. Or Sofia. Or Grace and Hope. Or Lizzy and Leon.

Her breath was hitching in her throat. This world, this relationship…her brain wouldn't let her believe it was all down to chance. To the pointing of a finger by a five-year-old.

'I need to know,' said Giovanni quietly. 'I need to know that we can have a relationship together. I need to know that you can accept me and Sofia as a package deal. I'm not asking you to give up your life in any way. We can talk about all that.' He took a deep breath and looked at her again. 'But I need to know that you can give me your heart—your whole heart—just like Sofia and I will give you ours.'

He took another breath, and when he looked at her she thought her heart might melt in her chest.

'Because I love you, Autumn. *We* love you. And I want nothing more than to find a way to make this work between us.'

Something twisted deep down inside her. She hadn't expected this conversation. Not now. Not here. Her stomach was instantly in knots. These were words she'd wanted to hear but wasn't entirely sure how to respond to.

'Before you say anything else, I want to be honest with you about something,' said Giovanni.

He looked troubled. Autumn's chest was tightening. She wanted to tell him that of course she loved him. That she could give him her whole heart. But that part…it was sticking.

'Wh-what is it?' she stammered.

Giovanni fixed his eyes on the horizon. 'You've probably heard people in the hospital talking about Anna.'

'Yes?' It came out as a question.

He ran his fingers through his hair again. She'd realised that he only ever did that when he was either nervous or frustrated. Which was it here?

'Most people had a picture-perfect view of our marriage. Which, for a time, might have been true. We grew up here. Met at the hospital. Fell in love, got married and had Sofia.'

The pain sitting on Autumn's chest seemed to deepen. She didn't need to hear this. She didn't need to hear about Giovanni's perfect life. People around the hospital mentioned Anna all the time, with a sad and reminiscent look in their eyes. It was hard not to feel a little hostile about it. How could she ever compete with a perfect memory…a perfect ghost?

'But things weren't like that. Hadn't been for a while, at least.' He hesitated, then straightened his shoulders. 'We…grew apart. And after Sofia's birth Anna was frustrated. With me…with life.'

Autumn frowned. 'She didn't like being a mother?'

Giovanni shook his head. 'No, not that. She loved Sofia entirely. But she felt trapped.' He put his hand to his chest. 'By me. We'd been talking about splitting before she fell pregnant. We stayed together *because* she was pregnant. I thought—I hoped—that things might get better, but they didn't. She decided to return to work early and told me she still wanted to leave the marriage.'

He shook his head again and Autumn watched him swallow.

'We kept our fights away from our colleagues at the hospital. When Anna died… I found it hard. I had to pretend that my wife and I had still been perfectly happy and in love, when nothing could have been further from the truth.'

Autumn felt frozen. The wave of relief that flowed over her at knowing that Giovanni hadn't been in love with his wife was shameful. And now she was wondering about the authenticity of the man in front of her. This was the man she'd contemplated trusting with her heart. If he'd fallen out of love with his wife, would he fall out of love with Autumn too?

She'd spent days questioning herself. Wondering why this gorgeous, hot Italian man seemed to have picked her, out of the hundreds of adoring women who were around him. Then she'd wondered why she couldn't just jump into his arms and dance around the corridors with him?

Was this why? Because she'd recognised something in his eyes on the few occasions he'd spoken about his wife? Maybe her subconscious had known he was hiding something from her? It could be that her instincts to hold on to her heart had been entirely correct.

Her fingers wound around a strand of her hair.

'I wanted to be honest with you—' His voice was gravelly.

'But you weren't,' she interrupted.

'I'm trying to be,' he said. 'I want us to have the best chance of making this work. That's why I want you to know everything I think you should know, before we take the next step.'

Her brain was numb. 'You've lived a lie these past few years.'

He shifted uncomfortably. 'But I'm the only person to know that. I had Sofia to think of.' He held out his hands. 'What kind of a guy speaks ill of his dead wife?' He actually shuddered as he said those words. 'And what was there to gain from telling everyone we would likely have split up had she not been killed? I want Sofia to remember good things about her mother. Surely that's not too much to ask?'

Autumn's throat was dry. 'But I'm not "everyone". I'm the woman who met your daughter. Who shared your bed. If you weren't honest about this—what else have you lied to me about?'

She could feel the layers wrapping around her. Wrapping around her to keep herself safe. This was exactly what she'd feared about letting go and losing control of things—especially her heart. She would swear it was physically twisting in her chest right now.

It was about much more than honesty. But she couldn't quite articulate that right now. The words seemed the simplest to say. But he'd told her he'd fallen out of love with his wife. A woman who had given her heart to him.

Fear swept around Autumn, and again those feelings of a lack of control circled around and around. She couldn't control how he felt about her. She'd never be able to do that. He said he loved her now—but for how long?

She already knew how she felt about him. But she couldn't tell him. She couldn't tell him how much she loved and adored him. Couldn't return those words. Not right now.

In her head she could see pictures of being wrapped up in a family life with Giovanni and Sofia, only for him to change his mind a few years later and leave her on her own. Empty and useless.

The thoughts overwhelmed her.

'I haven't lied to you about anything, Autumn,' he said softly. 'I wouldn't do that. I didn't lie to you about this either. I wanted to take the time to get to know you. To know that I truly wanted to make this work between us. Because I think we can make a go of things. And I'm telling you now because I want to start this relationship with all my cards on the table.'

He was talking, saying words she wasn't really hearing. All she could think about was the myth that followed Giovanni around about him and his wife. It didn't matter that she'd found the whole thing intimidating anyway, and wondered how she could ever live up to the stories about his perfect wife. All that mattered was that it had all been an illusion. They hadn't been in love. Not when she'd died.

Did she really want to take a risk on something she had no control over? The future was so uncertain. Who was to say that in a few years' time he wouldn't want to walk away from her too? To take himself and Sofia back out of the life that she loved and leave her alone? She'd never risked her heart before—could she really do so now? It would be easier just to pull back, to insulate her heart the way she always had. To protect herself from any pain.

Flashes of her parents came into her head. Her brother had had the same upbringing as herself. He'd walked his own way, turned his life around and taken a million chances. He was happier now than she'd ever known him to be. But deep down Autumn knew that she didn't have faith in herself, or now in Giovanni, to do the same.

She shook her head and backed away.

'Autumn, don't do this.' His face looked stricken. As if he'd just realised what his words had done.

She kept on shaking her head. 'No. This won't work. I can't trust you.' She stared at him for a second. 'You fell out of love with your wife—how do I know you won't fall out of love with me? I can't do this.'

Every cell in her body was telling her to run. To get away. To keep herself safe and not open herself up to the level of hurt that was already tearing at her soul.

Giovanni squeezed his eyes closed for a minute and she could see his hands shaking.

'We need to talk about this more,' he said.

She held up her hand firmly in front of his face. 'No.' Her voice was firm and clear. 'We don't.'

His gaze met hers. It was as if shutters were falling down across his eyes. He looked as though she'd just stabbed him in the heart.

'We can't do this now...' There was a tremble in his voice.

'You're right. We can't.'

The girls. They were too important. The surgery was critical. Neither could walk away from this. They had a duty and a responsibility to perform the separation surgery and subsequent surgeries with no distractions.

This wasn't about them. This had never been about them.

She held up her head, not meeting his gaze. 'I came here with one purpose: to help save the lives of Grace and Hope. That's all that matters here.'

The words were breaking her heart, even though it was she who was saying them out loud. It was as if she trying to switch parts of herself off. If she said all this, it might convince her that she hadn't already let Giovanni and his daughter capture those parts of her heart she'd tried so hard to keep in her control.

Tears were forming in her eyes and she was

determined not to shed them. But Giovanni's next words felt like a lance through her heart.

'You're absolutely right. This is about Hope and Grace. This has to be about Hope and Grace.'

She could hear the tinge of regret in his voice.

'I'm sure that you and I can conduct ourselves like the professionals we both are and do the very best for our patients.'

She hated him. In that second, she actually hated him. It didn't matter that she could see the pain in his eyes right now. She couldn't think about him and how he was feeling. She couldn't think about how he'd told her that he loved her and opened up to her completely. Her legs had turned to jelly. Her priority had to be to get out of here before she fell completely apart.

'Agreed.' That was all she could manage before she turned and walked down the corridor, wishing she was anywhere else but in Rome.

Love wasn't for her. Happy-ever-after wasn't for her. She should have known better and continued to live her life the way she always had. The risks were just too great, and she didn't have the courage to take that final step into the unknown.

CHAPTER TWELVE

It was amazing how easy it was to avoid someone in the hospital. He would enter a room and she would leave it. Both with smiles on their faces, and both giving no sense to those around them that there were any issues. That was what being a professional was. And, although every glance in his direction hurt, every time she heard the sound of his voice or, even worse, the echo of his laugh, she lifted her chin and kept going.

They communicated, of course. Emails back and forth about Hope, Grace and any logistics.

She'd left some test results on his desk with a query that he'd answered promptly. He, in turn, had left her a picture of a female doctor wearing a superhero cape that Sofia had drawn for her. There had been a note.

Sofia insisted I brought you this today. Would you mind sending her a text via my phone to let her know you've got it?

Tears had definitely been in her eyes at that point, as she'd admired the dark-haired, red-caped woman who looked as if she could move mountains.

She'd dashed off a text.

Sofia, thank you so much for my superhero picture. I absolutely love it! Xxx

She'd told herself she could do this. This wasn't about her and Giovanni. This was about the little girl whom she spent most days thinking about.

At night she sat in her hotel room with the doors wide, looking out at Rome. She'd stopped drinking alcohol, always aware that her pager might sound at any moment. Instead she would nibble on whatever food she'd found from a take-away, and drink from a bottle of sparkling water, and contemplate what might come next.

No matter how hard she tried, all those thoughts focused around Giovanni and Sofia and the lives they had here.

Her brother called late one night, to check up on her. 'You haven't messaged me yet. When's the surgery? I keep checking every day.'

She sighed and ran her fingers through her damp hair as she walked through from the bathroom. 'Any day. Literally any moment. The girls are doing okay. There're a few things I'm worried about, but the longer we can give them, the bigger they'll get. They're breathing with only nasal oxygen support and seem to be tolerating their feeding tubes. If they could keep going for another two weeks that would be fantastic. But to be honest I think we'll need to do the surgery before then.'

'And how's Rome? What about the guy—the other surgeon? You sounded so happy last time we spoke. Should I buy a hat?'

Her stomach sank like a stone, and he picked up on her silence immediately. 'Has something happened?'

'He's just not who I thought he was,' she said finally.

Her brother took a few moments before he replied. 'He sounded pretty good last time we spoke...'

He let the words hang there.

Autumn couldn't think what to reply.

'Sis, there was something different this time. I've never heard you talk about someone like that ever—in all the years I've known you.'

'I must have,' she said dismissively.

'No, you haven't.' His response was firm.

'What are you trying to say?'

She was getting annoyed now. It had all been so easy for Ryan. He'd met the woman of his dreams at a summer camp in America when he'd been nineteen. They'd just 'clicked'. Miriam had been there when Ryan had made the discovery that had made him a billionaire, and they'd remained in their happy little bubble ever since.

Ryan breathed in deeply. 'I'm saying I'm sorry I left you with Mr and Mrs Perfect. I guess I didn't quite understand that me escaping left you as the focus for their whole attention.'

Her skin prickled uncomfortably. There was so much they didn't need to say to each other. 'They weren't so bad,' she said, with no confidence.

'Yes, they were. You proved just how clever you were and got out to become the brilliant surgeon that you are. But, Autumn, life isn't perfect. I sometimes worry that the guys you've met over the years are the easy ones. The pleasant, mediocre guys you think will give you an easy life, rather than the guys that would just blow you away in a heartbeat.'

She was stunned. Ryan didn't normally say things like that.

'I love you, Sis. But sometimes you need to take a chance on something. Go for it, whether it might work or not.'

'But that's crazy.'

'It can also be fun, and the best experience of a lifetime, whether it lasts or not.'

But those words left her chilled. She wanted guarantees. She didn't want to take chances.

'Not for me,' she said sadly.

She heard a noise in the background. 'Give me a minute!' she heard Ryan call, then, 'Okay, I need to run. But two words to think about.'

'What?'

'Learned behaviour. Think about it. And text me when you do the surgery. I want to hear all about it.'

The phone went dead and Autumn made a grab for her bottle of water, her throat instantly dry. *Learned behaviour.* He was talking about their parents and their controlling.

She stood up and started pacing, shaking out her still damp hair. No. She didn't want to think about that—to contemplate any of that. She flopped down onto the bed and picked up the room service menu.

Two minutes later she'd ordered one of everything from the dessert menu. Anything to distract her from actually examining the fact that she'd never got to shout, scream and play as a child, and that had turned her into the repressed adult she was now.

No one else had challenged her to have these sorts of feelings. No one else had pushed her to strive for a life and a love that had always been kept a comfortable distance away. Just a too-handsome Italian with electrifying stubble and deep, deep brown eyes.

As far as Autumn was concerned, those desserts couldn't come quickly enough.

CHAPTER THIRTEEN

THREE VERY AWKWARD days later, Autumn walked into Giovanni's office just as he was replacing the phone, to ask him to take a look at one of the latest scans. The blood supply to Hope and Grace's liver was looking more compromised by the day.

He'd just stood up when their pagers went off simultaneously. It was like Groundhog Day.

One glance at her waistband told her everything she needed to know.

Giovanni was quicker, but Autumn was on his heels.

The hospital staff appeared to have a sixth sense, and all slid back against walls to allow their sprint to the ICU.

Giovanni burst through the doors. 'What's wrong?'

Agatha, one of the nurses looked up. 'It's Hope. Her blood pressure is crashing.'

'Page Team Hope and Team Grace. Surgery

is *now*.' The words were out of Autumn's mouth in an instant.

It was the oddest thing, but Autumn had experienced this in hospitals all over the world. In the most proficient units the worst-case scenario didn't send staff into a panic. It actually made them quiet, and they became the most organised people on the planet.

Agatha signalled to another nurse. 'We're going directly to Theatre. Come with me.'

A member of the admin team held her hand up at the desk. 'Paging everyone and dialling Theatre.'

One of the more junior doctors started unplugging equipment around the incubator to allow transportation.

Giovanni locked gazes again with Autumn. 'Do you want to go ahead and scrub?'

She shook her head. 'No. We'll *both* take our girls to Theatre.' She emphasised the word 'both'. It was a message. They were in this together.

Autumn licked her lips and closed her eyes, taking a few seconds for what lay ahead.

'Where are Gabrielle and Matteo?'

Agatha spoke clearly. 'I sent a member of staff to find them as soon as I'd paged you both.'

Autumn nodded. 'We start moving now. Your member of staff brings them to the theatre doors.

Reassure them that they'll get to see their babies before we start.'

The next two minutes were frantic. As they moved into the elevator Giovanni started another infusion for Hope. By the time the doors opened at the corridor to theatre Izi, one of the anaesthetists, was waiting for them, slightly out of breath.

'Fill me in,' was all he said.

Neither Giovanni nor Autumn started to speak. They let Agatha give a report of the circumstances that had led her to page them.

'Something's bleeding, then,' said Izi, reaching the same conclusion as everyone else. 'We stabilise as best we can and start the surgery?'

Giovanni and Autumn nodded in unison.

Her heart was racing in her chest. This was it. This was the surgery she'd come here for. And this wasn't the set of circumstances she'd wanted. An hour ago the girls had been stable. But they'd always known this could happen. The surgery had been scheduled for next week. They'd hoped for the girls to be a little stronger.

Some of their teams were already scrubbing as they reached the theatre.

Autumn noticed that the theatre next to theirs was still in session. 'How long?' she asked over her shoulder.

The theatre manager appeared behind her. 'Twenty minutes.'

Everyone knew that ultimately, they would need two theatres. Once the separation was completed, Hope and Grace would go into theatres of their own, where Giovanni would complete the necessary surgery on Hope, and Autumn would carry out the painstaking surgery on Grace. Part of her brain told her that this surgery could end up in the record books for its length and complexity, but these were things she couldn't think about right now.

There was a voice next to her. Asta—the theatre sister she'd appointed as her team leader for this surgery.

'Autumn, the parents are here. While you and Giovanni talk to them I'll do a check for all staff. Because it's short notice, some might not have got here yet. I'll get you a timeline for everyone.'

That was what she needed. Efficiency. And that was exactly why she'd picked Asta for her team.

She looked up from where she was scrubbing. Giovanni was in the same position as she was. Both had their gowns and caps in place; both were ready to put on their surgical gloves.

The lives of these little girls were at stake. But they had to make room for the parents too. Both she and Giovanni understood that this might be the last chance for Gabrielle and Matteo to see their babies alive.

She lifted her hands in front of her, careful to touch nothing. Giovanni did the same.

'I'll get the doors,' said one of the theatre orderlies.

They moved to the anaesthetic room, where Izi was with the girls and had allowed the parents in to see them as he monitored carefully. *One minute,* he mouthed to them both.

They understood.

'What's happened?' asked Matteo, his eyes bright with tears.

Autumn spoke softly. 'We think they're bleeding somewhere inside. We have to take them to Theatre to try and fix the problem.'

Gabrielle sniffed as she stroked both Hope and Grace's arms. 'You said this could happen.'

Giovanni started talking, defaulting into Italian. Autumn picked up most of what he was saying and was proud of herself.

He spoke plainly. 'Kiss your girls,' he told them. 'I promise you, we will do our absolute best.'

Tears brimmed in Autumn's eyes too. This situation was totally outside their control, and she couldn't imagine how terrified they were right now.

She nodded in agreement with Giovanni as

Matteo and Gabrielle kissed their daughters and left the room, terrified.

'I have staff assigned to them for the whole time you're in Theatre,' said the neonatal manager from the door. 'Page me.'

She didn't need to say the words. They all knew what she meant.

Giovanni and Autumn went back through to the scrub room.

'Are you ready for this?' Giovanni asked, his eyes dark and serious.

'Are you?' she replied.

His reaction was automatic. He took a step towards her. For the briefest moment their foreheads rested against each other, hands held outwards to avoid touching.

'We've got this,' she whispered, but she wasn't quite sure if she was saying it for him or for them both. She was downright terrified.

'We have,' he replied, sucking in a deep breath before lifting his head and stepping back.

As she headed to the theatre door his voice was deep behind her.

'And when all this is done we need to talk again. I'm not ready to let you go.'

She didn't react. She couldn't react. But it was as if he was reaching a hand out towards her.

His words soothed her soul and gave her hope. She was stepping into Theatre with a man she needed to trust implicitly. He knew that. And this was his olive branch.

'Autumn?'

Asta appeared at her elbow, a checklist of over twenty staff in her hand. She knew that Giovanni's team leader would be mirroring her actions.

'We have a problem.'

Words that Autumn didn't want to hear.

Her heart jumped. 'What's the problem?'

'Daniel.'

Giovanni lifted his head from the other side of the room, obviously in tune with their conversation.

'What's wrong with Daniel?' she asked, desperately not wanting to hear the answer.

Asta's face was grave. 'I've just spoken to him. He has gastroenteritis. Just in the last few hours. He can't come anywhere near the theatre.'

Her bright light. Her second in command. It was the worst news she could hear.

'You can have Akio.'

Akio was Daniel's equivalent on Giovanni's team. A superb surgeon. The temptation to say yes and grab him with both hands was strong.

'But he's done all that specialist training for your team,' she said. 'He should be used where his expertise is best.'

'He's adaptable,' said Giovanni.

She could hear the reluctance in his voice, and she completely understood why.

'There is another option,' said Asta softly.

'Who?'

'Ricardo. He hasn't done this exact surgery, but he's performed similar over the years.'

Autumn swallowed. Ricardo. The older surgeon she'd argued with Giovanni over, saying he wasn't quite good enough to be on any team. Giovanni had eventually reluctantly agreed with her.

Izi shouted from the theatre. 'Get in here, people, we need to start.'

Panic gripped her chest. Things were slipping out of her control. She'd picked her team carefully, ensuring there were no weak links. Part of her brain hated it that she considered Ricardo a weak link, but it was her job as lead surgeon to make that call.

Her brain scanned every other possible candidate. There were a few possibilities. But none had the previous surgical experience of Ricardo.

'Are there any models left?'

Asta frowned, but nodded.

'Okay, we'll be in here for a few hours. I'll need Ricardo for the second surgery. Can you call him and ask him to practise upstairs until we need him?'

Was that really cheeky? Maybe. But he hadn't been involved for the last few weeks. Grace's liver was basically going to be shredded. The model up in the clinical room showed the extent of the problem. It would also give him a good idea of the vein retrieval that was required.

She was swallowing her panic as best as she could. Her eyes met Giovanni's. He gave her a simple nod.

'Trust Ricardo,' he said quietly.

She couldn't see his mouth. Only his eyes.

She felt a flicker of panic starting to creep around her. She could do this. She could do this surgery with no assistance. But it would be long and arduous. Even she might get tired. The only person who expected her to be invincible was herself.

'Ask him,' she said to Asta. 'Then I need you back here with me.'

Asta gave the briefest of nods before disappearing.

Izi was positioned at the head of the table. Both girls were now anaesthetised. 'We're ready,' he said.

Autumn locked eyes with Giovanni. There was a gleam in his eye, a confidence in both himself, and in her.

She smiled underneath her mask. 'Let's do this.'

* * *

One surgery merged into the next. Every bone and muscle fibre in his body ached. He ignored the people watching the pioneering surgery from the gallery above them and focused only on Grace and Hope.

When they made the final incision to separate the girls, the whole room hushed.

Autumn leaned over and stroked both girls' faces and spoke in the sweetest voice he'd ever heard.

'Grace, Hope, we're going to keep you apart for a little while—just to make sure you both get better. But as soon as we can we'll have you next to each other again. I promise you that.'

Her bright green eyes locked with his and he could see the raft of emotions hidden behind the mask.

He spoke quietly too. 'Okay, Hope, you're going to stay with me, while Grace goes next door.' He touched the tiny dark hairs on Grace's head. 'See you soon, beautiful.'

And in the blink of an eye he was in Theatre with only his team.

Hope's surgery was quicker than Grace's. It was still painstaking and intricate work, but his team were well-practised and things went like clockwork. Six hours later he finished the neat row of stitches in Hope's abdomen and chest.

He took a moment, leaning back over her. 'All done, sweetheart. Now I'm going to see your sister while my colleagues look after you.'

He looked over his shoulder and through to the adjoining theatre. He could see Autumn, her strain evident in the set of her jaw and stiff shoulders.

'What's happening?' he asked, his focus shifting for the first time in hours.

The ICU sister was getting ready to transfer Hope. 'I think they had an issue with the vein retrieval,' she said. 'They had to change plans.'

His stomach clenched. Autumn had practised that part of the surgery over and over again. He tried to stay calm as he wondered how the lack of control was messing with her mind.

She was a professional. She had assistance. He should have faith in her. But he wanted to burst in and ask if she needed assistance. Every part of his body wanted to help the woman he loved.

'Giovanni?'

The ICU sister was looking at him expectantly.

'Matteo and Gabrielle? Are you coming to update them?'

Of course. That had to be his first priority.

He snapped off his gloves. 'Absolutely.'

He took one last glance over his shoulder and then followed his team out of the theatre.

* * *

She was calm. She was definitely calm. But she'd noticed the movement next door. 'Have they finished?'

'They have,' replied one of the theatre team who was standing against the wall.

'How did things go?'

'Just as expected. Hope's good and being transferred to ICU.'

Autumn took a few long, slow breaths. Hope was good. The surgery had been a success. She'd expected it, but was still surprised at the huge wave of relief rolling over her right now.

Ricardo's grey gaze caught her attention. He had his instruments poised carefully. There was a hint of hostility in the air between them that both were choosing to ignore. He clearly knew that she was the reason he hadn't been chosen for a team. But when he'd been called today, he'd come immediately. And he'd practised for a few hours in the lab upstairs.

She wondered if she would have been as forgiving.

Now he spoke in a low voice, showing parts of experience, resentment and knowledge. 'The radial artery is unsuitable. We'll need to use the saphenous vein.'

'Have you done this before?' asked Autumn.

In adult coronary artery bypass surgery, the

artery in the arm, or the vein in the leg, were often the vessels used to replace damaged cardiac vessels. To give Grace's liver a blood supply she'd always known they would have to do a similar kind of surgery. But all her thoughts had been based on using the radial artery.

'Have you?' queried Ricardo.

Autumn swallowed. If they couldn't repurpose a suitable artery or vein, then Grace wouldn't survive this surgery. Her tiny lobe of liver wouldn't have a chance to heal and grow. But she wasn't going to let the panic that was trying to creep up and over her get a hold. Certain elements of this were outside her control, but she had to grasp the parts that she still had. Starting with Ricardo.

She heard a noise as the door opened. Giovanni. He moved as if it were the most normal thing in the world to come into another surgeon's theatre during a ground-breaking operation. He grabbed one of the wheeled stools and perched a leg on it, pushing back against the wall and folding his arms.

He was here for the long haul. She knew that. He wasn't going to interfere. He wasn't going to offer to help. But if she needed him to assist all she had to do was ask. It was like a warm comfort blanket being nestled on her shoulders.

She sucked in a breath and counted in her

head, pushing the panic away from her. 'Ricardo,' she said steadily. 'Give me your professional opinion on whether the saphenous vein is the best option or whether we should consider something else.'

It was a question she would never normally ask in her theatre. She was the lead surgeon. This was her surgery. But she was willing to do whatever it took to make things work here today and give Grace the best possible outcome. If that meant she had to mend bridges with a surgeon she'd offended, then she would absolutely do that. Grace was what mattered.

There was silence for a minute. She tried to work out if Ricardo was being rude, or if he was genuinely taking the time to think. When his grey eyes met hers, he gave her the smallest of nods. He'd appreciated being asked for an opinion.

'Here's what I think we should do,' he said…

Nine hours later Autumn tugged the heart-covered cap from her sweaty head, the mask from her face, and walked around the table and kissed Ricardo on both cheeks. 'Fabulous!' she exclaimed.

There had been more than a few heart-stopping moments. Ricardo was much older than her, and at one point Giovanni had wheeled over his stool to let him sit for a few minutes' rest. The support had helped, and Ricardo had continued his part of the surgery with the stool adjusted to the height of the operating table, allowing him to lean over Grace's tiny body.

As Grace was whisked quickly away to ICU, Autumn stood in the theatre for a few moments with her hands on her hips.

The rest of the staff quickly disappeared until it was just her and Giovanni. His mask and cap were gone too.

'You have to speak to Gabrielle and Matteo,' he said slowly.

She nodded, knowing how important it was to let them know that the surgery had been a success. But that didn't help the way her heart was currently twisting inside her chest. Her part was over. She could stay for the recovery, and stall for however many weeks she wanted. But at the end of the day she would have to leave Rome.

And until this second she hadn't realised just how devastating that would be.

Slowly but surely her senses had started to awaken. She missed Sofia—the unpredictable five-year-old who also terrified parts of her. She missed her broad smile, her chatter, and the way she acted as though she'd been here before. She missed the way she could turn every book she read into a story about herself. And she missed the way Giovanni looked at his daughter when she did all those things.

Could she really face a life without seeing them both again?

Giovanni was looking at her. He'd said that after this they needed to talk. But talking was the last thing she wanted to do.

After years of living life by the rules. Of always being in control. Of never doing anything controversial or outlandish. Autumn knew entirely what she had to do next.

She held out her hand to Giovanni. 'Let's talk to the parents, and then I need you to come somewhere with me.'

He nodded, but glanced at her curiously as he stared at the clock on the wall. 'It's late—' he began.

She grabbed hold of his hand. 'I don't care what time it is. We'll speak to Gabrielle and Matteo, make sure everything is good with the girls, then we have to go.'

Giovanni was smiling, but his face was etched with amusement. 'Is this good or bad? Or shouldn't I ask?'

She grinned. 'Without a doubt, it's very, very bad.'

CHAPTER FOURTEEN

THEY HADN'T EVEN taken the time to change out of their scrubs. As soon as they'd spoken to the parents, and assured them everything was in place, Autumn had grabbed his hand and started pulling him down the corridor.

'Have you got your car keys?' she asked.

He nodded and pulled them from his pocket.

She dabbed something into her phone and then turned it around so he could see. 'Do you know where this is?'

'Of course.'

'Then that's where we're going.'

As they approached the main exit of the hospital it was clear that the weather was against them. Thunder sounded and lightning flashed across the sky. It wasn't just raining, it was pouring—a complete and utter deluge.

Giovanni stopped walking. 'I can't remember the last time it rained like this.'

He looked out in horror, but Autumn pulled

him along. She smiled. 'It's like being home in Scotland. This is normal.' Then she paused and tilted her head, the smile spreading even further. 'Maybe it's a message for me,' she said quietly.

'What?'

'Let's go.'

She yanked him through the front doors and out into the lashing rain. He started running across the car park towards his car, but she let go of his hand, holding her arms out and throwing her head back as she spun around a few times.

'Are you crazy?' he shouted, barely hearing his own voice above the thunder.

'Maybe!' She laughed as she joined him at the car.

They were already soaked as he started the engine and wove his way through the streets. 'Are you going to tell me what's going on?'

She shook her head. Speckles of water splattered from her hair. 'Just drive.'

He did as he was told, wondering what on earth was happening. It was late. As they glided up towards their destination the rain was still sheeting around them and the streets were empty of traffic.

'Here you are,' he said as he pulled the car over. 'Fontane del Tritone.'

Autumn pressed her face up against the window. 'It looks almost magical,' she whispered, her breath steaming the glass.

Giovanni killed the engine. The fountain was in the middle of a *piazza*—usually it was surrounded by traffic, but at this time of night, and in this weather, they seemed to be the only ones around. Lights on the fountain made the water gleam bright blue, and in the centre was the mighty Triton, his arms holding a conch to his lips, standing on four dolphin fins, with a rush of water spurting upwards from the conch.

In the dramatic black and purple background of the weather, the lit fountain did look magical.

'Let's go!' She grinned as she opened the door.

'And do what?' He still wasn't exactly sure what was going on.

But Autumn was already walking backwards towards the fountain. 'If I'm going to learn how to play and have fun, I might as well start somewhere good!'

She threw her arms apart again, spinning around before jogging towards the fountain. Her scrubs were instantly plastered to her skin, and he glanced quickly around to check for any traffic before sprinting after her. Before he had a chance to say anything she reached down and pulled her scrub top over her head.

'Autumn! What are you doing?'

'Living life!'

She swung her scrub top above her head. He ducked as he moved closer to her. Her dark hair was soaked, flattened against her head. Her pale skin glowed in the street lights. Her green eyes were gleaming as he put a hand at her waist.

Her breathing was fast. 'You asked me if I'd ever danced in the rain…jumped in a fountain? And my answer to everything was no. I'd never even considered any of those things. They were silly. They were ridiculous. But you've made me realise that if I want to love, if I want to have the life I long for, then I have to learn how to live first. I have to take risks…take chances. The things that have terrified me all my life. And I have to learn how to have fun.' She pressed her wet nose against his. 'Wanna have some fun with me?'

Before he had a chance to answer she threw her hands in the air and jumped into the fountain, kicking and splashing as she whooped out loud.

His head was spinning. He *had* said those things. Never realising just how literally she'd take them. But inside, his heart was exploding with joy. She was doing this for him. She was doing this for them.

There was nothing else for it. He jumped into the fountain with her, joining her in the splashing. She started singing. A kid's song. He joined in, laughing as she danced around the dolphins.

It only took one minute for a car to slow down as it drove past, with two people staring in complete confusion through the windows.

Giovanni grabbed her again around the waist and pulled her to him. 'Autumn, you don't have to do this for me.'

She shook her head as she laughed and put her hands on his shoulders. 'I'm doing it for me first and you second. I love you, Giovanni, and I love Sofia too. And that, and you, and Sofia—all of it—still...' she tilted her head back and shouted to the dark sky '...*terrifies* me!'

As she straightened her head he could see tears on her face as well as the sheeting rain.

'But this is it. This is my chance to let go of controlling everything in my life and take a chance. Take a chance on me, on you, on us and life.'

She ran her hands through his sodden hair and moved her lips next to his ear. 'You trusted me, Giovanni. You told me about your wife, your truth and your fears. You told me you'd fallen out of love with her. And I backed away. I backed away because I was scared. Scared that if I gave my heart to you the same thing might happen. That I might spend years loving both you and Sofia and then you might fall out of love with me and walk away.' She put her hand to her chest. 'I was already scared to take the risk, take the leap of loving you both. Don't you know I can't control that? I can't control how you both feel about me?'

'I love you, Autumn. I wanted us to start straight. The last thing I wanted to do was scare you off.' He put his hand to the side of her head. 'Why on earth would you ever think I might fall out of love with you?'

She put her hand on his chest. 'Because there's always that chance. That's what life is about. I've never met anyone like you. I've never felt anything like this before. I was scared that I might not be the person who could let herself love you the way you deserve to be loved.' Tears were pouring down her face, but she was smiling. 'My parents would be horrified by this behaviour. You told me to dance in the rain, jump in a fountain, and you were right. I have to let the world do what it needs to do around me. I can't control every little thing, and I have to take chances.' Her head dipped. 'I've missed out on so much because I was scared to take a chance on things.'

When he spoke his voice was deep, but shaking with emotion. 'Then I'm honoured that I'm the first guy you've danced with in the rain. That

Sofia and I are the people you want to take a chance on.'

A car tooted on its way past. In a far part of the *piazza* a couple huddled under an umbrella...one of them looked as if he might be on his phone.

'There's one thing we still need to do.' He cupped her cheeks in both hands and kissed her nose. 'This adventure isn't over yet.'

Now it was Autumn's turn to look confused. 'What?'

'It's a secret.' He grabbed her hand. 'But let's go before we get arrested.'

They ran back to the car, where Autumn grabbed her top and pulled it over her head again before they dived back in, soaking the seats with their wet scrubs. Giovanni blasted the heaters as he manoeuvred around the Rome streets. He was still grinning at her. Autumn peeled the scrub top from her skin, holding it out to try and keep some of the water from pooling on the seat.

Her nose wrinkled as he stopped the car and she pressed her nose to the window again. 'Where are we?'

'Just where we need to be.'

The rain hadn't lessened as he led her across the grass in one of the parks in Rome.

She laughed out loud when he sat down on the grass. 'Which one of us is crazy?'

He patted the sodden earth next to him. 'You said you wanted to play. We are going to play.' He held out his hands and tipped his head back. 'A bit of wet weather isn't going to stop us.'

Autumn looked completely confused. But, 'Okay...' she said as she sat down beside him. 'Anything for the man I love.'

Giovanni didn't doubt for a second that he was doing entirely the right thing. He plucked a few simple flowers from the grass and used his short nail to split each of the stems, then threaded them together.

Autumn bent her head close to his, dripping even more water over his delicate operation. Her shoulders started to shake. When her gaze met his, her eyes were gleaming. 'You're making me a daisy chain?'

He shook his head. 'Oh, no. This is special. This is the first time I've ever done this. I'm making you...' he held it out '...a daisy ring.'

She stopped laughing, her eyes wide.

Giovanni took her trembling left hand. 'Autumn Fraser, will you do me the honour of making a life with me, and with my daughter—wherever that will be in the world—and filling our lives with love and joy for ever?'

She didn't hesitate for a second, throwing her arms around his neck. 'You have my complete heart,' she whispered in the rain. 'Take care of it. I can't afford for it to be broken. But somehow…' she pulled back and ran her finger down his cheek and beard '… I think I've picked the perfect keeper for my heart.'

She held out her hand and he delicately placed the now slightly squashed daisy ring on her finger. 'You should know,' he said quietly, 'that not only did Sofia pick you, she also told me I had to give you a daisy ring when we got engaged.'

He couldn't wipe the smile from his face. The longest day of his life had turned into the best.

'The girl's got taste,' laughed Autumn. 'And now,' she said, and shook her head, 'would you do me a favour and take me home?'

'It will be my pleasure,' said Giovanni, and they walked slowly, covered in bits of grass and mud, back to the car and into their new life together.

EPILOGUE

HER BROTHER HAD insisted on paying for the wedding and flying all the guests to the venue—his castle in Scotland. Today Scotland had been blessed with good weather and the sun was high in the sky.

Sofia was beside herself. 'I'm a princess,' she kept saying as she twirled around in the cream satin dress with a peach waistband that she'd chosen herself. 'Are we ready now?' She was bouncing on her toes and glancing out at the people in the gardens beneath their room.

Autumn smiled down at her engagement ring. The central yellow diamond was surrounded by glistening white diamonds, and looked as near to a daisy as possible. Giovanni had presented her with the specially commissioned ring a few months after their daisy chain engagement.

'There's Lizzy and Leon and their baby!' said Sofia. A few moments later she turned with a deep frown. 'My aunties are fighting.'

She laughed, 'Ooh, Eleonora and Bella have the same colour on!'

Autumn tried to stifle a grin as she finished fastening her rose gold earrings—a wedding gift from Giovanni. She stood up and smoothed down her own satin gown, straightening the peach tie that matched Sofia's around her waist.

She picked up her bouquet of peach roses and handed the smaller version to Sofia. 'We're ready to go now.'

Sofia ran back to the window. 'Daddy's there!'

Autumn's heart fluttered. She couldn't believe she'd actually reached this moment, when she would give herself wholeheartedly and completely without fear of losing control.

It hadn't come easily. Losing a lifetime of learned habits and behaviours had taken time. She'd had some counselling, and Giovanni and her brother had been with her every step of the way.

She bent down in front of Sofia. 'I can't wait to marry you and your *papà*,' she said sincerely, trying not to cry and ruin her make-up. 'It's going to make me the happiest person on the planet.'

Sofia was grinning and she flung her arms around Autumn's neck. 'You're my best friend,' she said with a few sniffs.

'And you're mine,' agreed Autumn. She

straightened up and held out her hand to Sofia. 'Let's go.'

They walked down the aisle with Autumn's brother at her other side. Matteo and Gabrielle Bianchi were in the third row, Hope and Grace on their knees. Both girls were still small, but clearly thriving. Autumn blew them both a kiss as she walked past.

Sofia took things very seriously, timing her steps and waiting until she reached the front before she gave a big sigh of relief, hugged her *papà*, then sat on the red carpet under the floral arch.

Giovanni beamed at his bride. 'You made it,' he whispered.

'You thought I might get lost?' she asked, and smiled at her handsome groom in his tailored grey suit.

'I know you like to keep me guessing,' he said as he leaned over and kissed her cheek, the short beard that she'd insisted he keep scratching her skin.

'Hey…' the celebrant laughed '…doesn't that come at the end?'

Giovanni put his hands on Autumn's satin-covered hips and pulled her close. 'Should we tell her?' he teased.

'I think so,' said Autumn as she put her hands on his shoulders.

They both turned at the same time. 'We'd like to start the way we mean to continue.'

Then they laughed, and kissed again, before the ceremony had even started.

* * * * *

If you missed the previous story in the Double Miracle at Nicollino's Hospital duet, then check out

A Family Made in Rome
by Annie O'Neil

And if you enjoyed this story, check out these other great reads from Scarlet Wilson

His Blind Date Bride
Family for the Children's Doc
Cinderella and the Surgeon

All available now!